G000141294

ALEXI NIKITIN was born in Kiev, Ukraine, USSR, in 1967.
He studied physics at Kiev University and spent time in
the army after which he worked in the gas and nuclear
industries – including devising an emergency system for
suppressing dust contamination from the Chernobyl
sarcophagus. He published his first story in 1990 and has
since published a number of novels and novellas. In
2000 he won the Ukrainian Writers Union Korolenko
Prize for the year's best work of fiction in Russian. *Istemi*
is his first work to be translated into English.

istemi

istemi

Alexei Nikitin

Translated by Anne Marie Jackson

PETER OWEN
London and Chicago

PETER OWEN PUBLISHERS
81 Ridge Road, London N8 9NP

Peter Owen books are distributed in the USA and Canada by
Independent Publishers Group/Trafalgar Square
814 North Franklin Street, Chicago, IL 60610, USA

Translated from the Russian *Istemi*

Originally published by Ad Marginem Press
under the title *Истеми* in Moscow 2011

English translation first published in Great Britain 2013
by Peter Owen Publishers

© Alexei Nikitin 2011
Translation © Anne Marie Jackson 2013

ISBN 978-0-7206-1464-0

A catalogue record for this book is available
from the British Library

Typeset by Octavo-Smith Ltd in Constantia 11.5/15
Display Engravers MT

Printed and bound in the UK by
CPI Group (UK) Ltd, Croydon, CR0 4YY

This publication was effected under the auspices of the
Mikhail Prokhorov Foundation TRANSCRIPT Programme
to support translations of Russian literature.

The translator is grateful to Vladimir Andreev, Inna Chuyeva, Olessia Makarenia, Tatiana Stepanova and Lydia Strong for generously sharing their time and expertise.

2004

My email address is istemi@ukr.net. Whenever I give it out over the telephone the other person is sure to ask 'Is what?' 'Istemi is a name,' I say and spell it out, 'I-S-T-E – ISTEMI.' An address such as davidov@ukr.net or adavidov@ukr.net would suit me better – my name is Alexander Davidov – but when I was setting up the account those addresses were already taken, and I didn't feel like messing around with numbers and coming up with something along the lines of davidov04. Then I thought of Istemi.

Istemi was the last sovereign ruler of the Khanate of Zaporozhye. He brought an end to the war with the Arab Caliphates, and during the Taman crisis he sacked Deputy Hetman Bagratuni and personally flew out to Tver to settle the dispute with Slovenorussia. Istemi wasn't afraid of losing face in front of President Betancourt, and as a result he won. He didn't win the war, no, but he won the peace. He was exacting towards the government and severe with the parliament. Sometimes I was afraid of him myself.

These days no one even remembers him. In the encyclopaedia you can read about another Istemi, the younger brother of Bumin. Fifteen centuries ago, backed by fifty thousand mounted Oghuz Turks, the brothers' tribe attacked the Rouran Khanate. The Rouran fell as readily as if it had been awaiting the brothers' appearance . . . and there and then the Khanate was resurrected under a new name. The new khan was Bumin. A year later Bumin died. He was succeeded first by one son then another. Bumin's offspring expanded the new empire in the east. They gained control over the Kyrgyz on the Yenisei, demanded tribute from the Northern Qi and the Northern Zhou and reached as far as the shores of the Yellow Sea. But, according to the law of the steppe, the heartland of the tribe remained with Bumin's younger brother Istemi. Istemi didn't quarrel with his nephews or struggle against them for power. He headed west, gathering tribes and states like windfall plums. He concluded a treaty with the Sassanid Emperor Anushirvan Khosrau – the Philosopher King – then attacked and routed the Confederacy of the Hephthalites to the east. Certain details of this war can be found in the Persian *Book of Kings*. Istemi's daughter married Khosrau and gave birth to crown prince Hormizd. The title of Yabgu Khan, King of the Hephthalites, remains part of the title of Istemi's descendants to this day. In alliance with Byzantium Istemi attacked Iran, then, without any allies, he attacked the Byzantine possessions along the Black Sea. Istemi reached as far as the Bosporus, invaded Crimea and laid siege to Khersones.

But Istemi did not take Khersones, and he soon left Crimea. His successors, however, remained in

Eastern Europe from then on. The Khanate alternately expanded its borders – reaching as far as the shores of the Adriatic to the west and the Baltic marshes to the north – then retreated from the onslaught of its neighbours into a scarcely distinguishable strip of land along the shores of the Black Sea. More than once it fell into enemy hands, and five centuries ago it lost its historic shrine, the ancient capital of the khans at the mouth of the Itil, now called the Volga. The name of the Khanate changed through time: Khazaria, Cimmeria, Zaporozhye. I might be confusing the Zaporozhian Istemi with his namesake in the encyclopaedia – to this day the history of the Zaporozhian Khanate is full of dark spots, which Russians euphemistically call 'white spots'. But no one is ever going to fill them in now.

The final ruler of the Khanate, Istemi, disappeared exactly twenty years ago. The Khanate's archive went missing at the same time. The circumstances of Istemi's disappearance were tragic for me and four other people. They led to serious upheavals for three of us, an incurable illness for the fourth, and the fifth seems to have perished. The mailbox istemi@ukr.net was opened in the name of Istemi, but I was the only one who used it.

I check my email twice a day. Early in the morning and in the evening. There's no particular reason for this other than it just works for me. In the morning I have my breakfast half listening to the news on television and sifting through all the mail that has accumulated overnight. Usually it's just spam and emails from friends now living in America. I get a lot of spam – I don't know where it all comes from. But there isn't much genuine mail. I discard the spam without looking at it, quickly read the mail and go to work. It's late when I come back home, and before I go to bed I check my account again. In the evening I get mail from friends over here and even more spam. I take my time over my evening mail, then I glance at the morning mail once again and go to sleep shortly afterwards. Because in the evening, after work, all I can do is sleep. Nothing more. I answer my mail on Sundays, all at once. It's just what's easiest for me.

Work eats up all my time. I promote American fizzy drinks. It's a tiresome, uninteresting job. I can't imagine anyone actually liking it. Maybe that's because I'm older than everyone else in our office. The young are gamblers – they see a career as a game. Bonuses, bonus points, career advancement . . . they're like dogs chasing a mechanical hare. They'll play along for five years or so, pursuing the hare, but then, like me, they'll start scratching their heads and wondering what they're wasting their time on. On helping a bunch of guys they've never even met to sell as many plastic bottles of sickly-sweet brown swill as possible – water with a bit of concentrate and masses of preservatives, flavourings and dyes . . . Wasting their time on that? Lots of people will start scratching their heads, but in the end it depends on the person. Most of them will sell fizzy drinks for the rest of their lives. The pay, mind you, is not to be sneezed at.

* * *

When I last checked my account there was an email addressed to Istemi. Not to me but to him personally: for the attention of His Majesty, the Khan of the Khanate of Zaporozhye. The email arrived in the morning, sent from a Hotmail address consisting of assorted letters and numbers which presumably made some sense to the account holder but which meant nothing to me. I was in a hurry to get to work, so I decided to wait until evening to read it. All day I regretted my decision, wondering who might have sent the email and what was being proposed to His Majesty.

I read it in the evening:

Rome

9 March 2004

Your Majesty, my dear brother

In the spirit of friendship, I am forwarding to you herewith a copy of my ultimatum to Slovenorussia.

Please accept my warmest regards, etc., etc.

Karl

Attached to the email was the ultimatum. I looked at it in astonishment, unable to believe I was seeing those words once more.

On Monday, the tenth of this month, the Imperial and Royal Government was compelled, through the offices of its Imperial and Royal Minister in Tver, to address the following to the Government of Slovenorussia:

Recent history has shown that there exists within Slovenorussia a revolutionary movement determined to detach from the Holy Roman Empire a number of its territories.

This movement, which came into existence under the very eyes of the Slovenorussian Government, at long last has reached such proportions as to be manifest outside the borders of the Confederation in the shape of acts of terrorism – a series of murders and attempted murders. The Government of the Slovenorussian Confederation has undertaken no measures to suppress this movement.

It has tolerated the criminal activity of various societies and organizations against the Empire, the unrestrained zeal of the press, the participation of officers and officials in revolutionary activities, unwholesome propaganda in educational establishments and, in short, it has tolerated all manner of activity which may incite within the population of Slovenorussia hatred towards the Empire and contempt of its institutions.

The developments detailed above do not permit the Government of the Holy Roman Empire to henceforth maintain the patient and long-suffering stance which it has adopted for years in the face of events begun first in Tver and thence propagated throughout the territory of the Empire.

On the contrary, these circumstances compel it to bring to an end all such activities that threaten the peace within the Empire. Towards the achievement of these ends the Government of the Holy Roman Empire finds it necessary to demand that the Slovenorussian

Government make an official statement to the effect that it condemns all propaganda directed against the Holy Roman Empire and that, as proof of the sincerity of this statement, it will withdraw all of its armed forces from the border of the Empire to the Marburg-Leibach-Trieste Line and return these cities, as well as the Istrian Peninsula, to the rightful possession of the Emperor of the Holy Roman Empire.

The Government of the Holy Roman Empire expects the answer of the Government of the Slovenorussian Confederation no later than six o'clock on Thursday evening, the eleventh of March of the current year.

I knew these words only too well. There was a time when I had read them repeatedly and knew them by heart. I had kept the yellowed sheets of writing paper on which the ultimatum was printed at our dacha, between pages 44 and 45 of an ancient issue of *Youth*, coverless and thick with dust.

The letter and appendix stayed hidden in the magazine for almost seven years. All that time I was afraid someone would find it, someone who was looking specifically for the ultimatum, or else that, one fine summer evening as darkness fell, the last remaining document connected to Istemi, Khan of Zaporozhye, would be used to kindle the family campfire – vodka, potatoes, the mournful strains of 'Black Raven' and the buzz of mosquitoes here for the warm season.

But nothing happened to the ultimatum at the dacha. I brought it home again in the early 1990s – by then it was no longer dangerous. But at home I lost it. There's no point describing just how hard I searched for it. Words are insufficient. Soon I moved to a new apartment, then another. The ultimatum – sent by Karl XX, Emperor of the Holy Roman Empire, to the President of the Slovenorussian Confederation, Stefan Betancourt, and copied to the President of the United Islamic Caliphates, Caliph Al-Ali, the Lama of Mongolia, Undur Gegen, the Khan of the Khanate of Zaporozhye, Istemi – the last and only remaining document, in my safekeeping, that referred to the history of those states had disappeared.

But evidently someone still had a copy. Who? I rang Kurochkin. Kurochkin didn't answer.

1984

Getting arrested, it seemed, was a bit of a laugh. At first. As long as the serious, remarkably similar faces that had suddenly surrounded me remained unfamiliar, as long as my grasp of the absurdity of the situation did not give way to an uneasy sense of reality, hard and irrefutable as stone, as long as I was freely able to feel and think, it was fun.

They began by searching the house. The search lasted twenty hours, even though all the Khanate documents they were looking for – diplomatic correspondence, reconnaissance reports, extracts from the government's annual report – were lying on the window ledge in three messy heaps and in a folder on my desk. All they had to do was neatly gather the papers together, put them in special canvas bags and seal the bags. It would have taken thirty minutes. Half an hour. As for the remaining nineteen and a half hours, they could have had some beer, or vodka if they wanted it. Mama would have boiled some potatoes, sliced up some sausage and got out a jar of pickled gherkins. My mother made the most wonderful pickled gherkins, with garlic and dill, cherry leaves on occasion, sometimes even blackcurrant leaves. So, instead of wallowing in the dust under the sofa, rapping at the walls and the floor, moving book-cases and taking down shelves without putting them back again, disturbing my books and underwear and old notebooks, instead of all that they could have munched on gherkins and burnt the tips of their fingers and tongues on tasty hot potatoes, drunk some beer and had a laugh. Afterwards they might have had a little nap. And all the while the sacks with the Khanate documents would just have been lying there, safely sealed and in the corner of the room. Then they would have woken up and gone off happily to work. Taking me with them.

They certainly took me with them. But they went away feeling bad-tempered, hungry and sleep-deprived. And I went with them feeling bad-tempered, hungry and confused. I didn't understand what was happening.

The interrogations began several days later. Major Sinevusov, round and sallow pink, alternately oozed oil and venom. Once he finished with formalities he asked me to draw him a map of the Zaporozhye Khanate. He handed me a light-blue topographic map, the kind used in schools, and a red marker, bright and moist.

'Roughly like this,' I said a few minutes later and handed the map back to him.

The red line demarcating the territory of the Khanate from adjacent states ran along the southern and western borders of Bulgaria, cut across Romania and Ukraine and headed east just north of the small border town of Kiev. From the confluence of the

Voronezh and the Don, the line followed the Don until it emptied into the Sea of Azov.

'Roughly like this, then . . . roughly like this . . .' The pores of Sinevusov's face were glistening with oil. He took a handkerchief and mopped his forehead, cheeks and neck. 'So that's the Khanate of Zaporozhye?'

I nodded.

'What about the capital? Why haven't you shown the capital?'

'The capital is Uman.'

'Uman?'

'Two million two hundred thousand inhabitants according to the 1980 census. Uman.'

'Uh-huh,' the major snorted. 'Put it on the map?'

I shrugged. 'Sure.'

'Uman – Two million two hundred thousand . . . So what else can you tell me? Pretend I've never heard anything about this state . . . which, in fact, I haven't. Tell me more.'

'What do you want me to say?' I asked uncertainly. 'That's all there is to the entire state.'

'Take your time,' he said. 'There's no hurry, right? Be thorough. Give me details. Let's begin with the way it's organized. What's the socio-political system?'

'Constitutional monarchy.'

'Excellent. A constitutional monarchy. Like Britain?'

'Not quite. Everyone knows that the British queen reigns but doesn't rule. The khan, however, wields real power, and his power is handed down by succession.'

'What an old-fashioned form of government you

have in your Khanate,' said Sinevusov, not quite asking but without drawing a conclusion either.

I wasn't going to argue, but I added, 'The prime minister is appointed by the khan but approved by the parliament. The laws are ratified by the parliament but approved by the khan.'

'Like I was saying,' Sinevusov nodded, 'an old-fashioned form of government. Very nineteenth century. Who's looking after the interests of the working class? Or the labouring peasantry? Hmm? Enough. We can discuss that later. Carry on. Population size? Key branches of industry?'

'The population is 118 million –'

'According to the 1980 census?'

'Yes.'

'Brilliant. Carry on.'

'It has a territory of one million one hundred thousand square kilometres. The state language is Zaporozhian –'

'Even its own language . . .'

'The monetary unit is the grivna. The state religion is Judaism.'

'You've got Jews living there?'

'No, Zaporozhians.'

'And the religion is Judaism?'

'Yes.'

The major exhaled heavily and wiped oil from his brow.

'Very well . . . Your Zaporozhians go to the syna-gogue and settle their debts in grivnas . . .'

'Actually religion and state are separate in the Khanate, although history has brought about precisely the situation you describe. Most Zaporozhians are Jews. You can't rewrite history.'

'*Really*?' said the major with far more emphasis than necessary. 'You're telling me?'

I looked around. 'Is there someone else here?'

'Stick to the subject,' said the major, disregarding my question. 'Back to the Zaporozhians. There's so much you can learn in the course of an ordinary interrogation. Now tell me about the Khanate's army. And its foreign policy.'

'The Khanate of Zaporozhye is economically and industrially developed. Per capita income is slightly higher than thirty thousand grivnas . . . I can't remember the exact figures, but they're in the papers somewhere.'

'Indeed.' The major nodded. 'How much is that in roubles?'

'I don't know.' I shrugged. 'We didn't value them in roubles.'

'What currency did you value them in?' There was a metallic edge to his voice, and the pores of his neck and brow oozed oil and venom at the same time. 'Dollars? Marks? Israeli shekels?'

'The Zaporozhian grivna is a hard currency. Other states can use grivnas to value their income and budgets. You're interrupting me a great deal.'

Sinevusov nodded and said drily, 'Carry on.'

'The Khanate of Zaporozhye has a strong economy and solid industry,' I repeated out of spite. 'Machine building, instrument design, chemicals and agriculture are all well developed. The army is one million strong.'

'One per cent of the population,' clarified the major.

'More or less. The arsenal includes nuclear weapons, platforms for launching weapons of all ranges. But on the whole the Khanate is peaceful and hasn't been at war for many years.'

'Yet it has territorial issues . . .'

He knew what he was talking about. Itil, the Khanate's ancient capital, had been captured five hundred years before by the Slovenorussians. But the Khanate wasn't going to fight over it.

* * *

At first one interrogation was very like another. It was like helping schoolchildren who were about to take an examination and whom I was helping to prepare. The children asked me questions, and I'd answer them; they'd write down my answers and ask me more questions. The first interrogations were almost exactly like exam-preparation sessions. I was tutoring my investigator, Major Sinevusov. And waiting for him to come to the point.

2004

A day went by before I managed to get hold of Kurochkin. Kurochkin was a big fish in our rather small pond. He was now a Member of Parliament, and five years ago he was a Member of Parliament, but in between, he had been First Deputy Premier – I beg your pardon, they now style themselves First Deputy Prime Minister, a splendid title that is the secret posthumous envy of all the Viceroys of India. Kurochkin now had a stake in a reputable bank, and for his sustenance he had been given a fund through which ethereal American dollars were pumped into decrepit Ukrainian industry.

I had to ring him from the office. Not good. Once a month our office receives a list from the telephone exchange of all the numbers we've dialled. Including numbers dialled from mobiles. If they noticed that I'd rung Parliament two days in a row they would start asking me all kinds of stupid questions. But only if they noticed. And that was pretty unlikely.

Which reminded me of a time when it hadn't taken days to get through to Kurochkin, when I knew by heart all the numbers where I might find him, and he knew mine just as well. We could meet up at any time and for any reason, and reasons weren't hard to find. We didn't even look for them. At school we'd been in the same class, sat at the same desk, prepared for examinations using the same textbooks. I called him Kurkin, usually just Kur. We were both in love with Natasha Belokrinitskaya, and our chances were an even nil. And we were both searched at the same time and arrested on the same day

'Kurochkin,' I said, when I was finally put through, 'have you received a letter?'

He didn't ask what kind of letter. Perversely he said, 'I just knew this was one of your idiotic jokes.' And sighed heavily. Meaning it was his lifelong burden to endure me and my jokes. Labourer. Defender of the People's Welfare. Victim of Davidov.

But it meant he'd received the letter.

'No, Kurochkin, it's not one of my jokes. It's someone else's joke. I thought you might know something.'

'Davidov,' the note of fatigue was gone, but the perversity remained, 'have you any idea how busy I am? Today alone I . . .' Here he yawned loudly and began shuffling familiarly through his parliamentary papers. As if he were about to read through the day's entire order of business from the lectern in Parliament.

'Enough! I believe you,' I said, interrupting so that he wouldn't actually start reciting all his business.

'And here you are with your letter,' concluded Kurochkin with satisfaction.

'It's not my letter. And the text – word for word, it's . . .'

'Well, yes . . .'

24

'It's exactly the same. I know because I know it by heart. The only difference is the date.'

'I noticed. So it wasn't you?'

'That's what I'm trying to say.'

At that he grew thoughtful, and there was certainly plenty to think about.

'Which email account was your letter addressed to?'

'My parliamentary email. Why?'

'Can someone outside of Parliament get hold of it?'

'It's pretty straightforward – it's open access.'

'So will you write back then?' I asked simply, incidentally, as if that's not why I had called in the first place.

'Write back? Me? Are you pulling my leg, Davidov?'

'Well, just imagine it's an email from one of your electorate. You do have voters, right? One voter's pension has been miscalculated, another hasn't received the tax credit he's due . . .'

'And a third sends an ultimatum.'

'By the way, it's already four o'clock.'

'So?'

'You have until six to write back. You've got another two hours.'

'And the third', Kurochkin suddenly roared, 'sends me an ultimatum signed by Emperor Karl and demands the withdrawal of troops before six o'clock . . . Where does he want troops withdrawn from?'

'Leibach.'

'From Ljubljana, in other words. And the return of Istria. It would look just great if I used my parliamentary

25

email to answer this . . . this . . . Words fail me, honestly.'

'Then use a different email address if that's the problem.'

'It's not the address. Don't play the idiot.' Kurochkin was already more composed. 'You know it's not the address.'

'Fine. Then let's think on it for a few days. OK? And talk later.'

'OK. Although . . . Well, you know where to find me.'

I knew he wanted to say one more time that he wasn't interested. But he didn't say it. And it's a good thing, too. Because I knew this was interesting and important. As important as it had been before, although twenty years had passed since it had all first begun.

1984

It's a long time since I've been able to believe myself. I don't believe what I remember. I'm sure that's not how it was . . . but how was it? I would be glad, I would even want to watch – right now, but as a bystander, an invisible observer in a far-away corner – what had actually happened. To hear again the questions I was asked and how I answered. Sinevusov's office with its window overlooking a courtyard, the lifeless fluorescent light in the cell . . . Scores of times I've seen them in dreams, hundreds of times in memory. Yet always afresh, always somehow different. For every minute of the interrogation, every day spent in that cold place, sequestered inside the concrete walls of the inner prison, away from the rest of the world, every minute and every day was different from all other minutes and days. And the differences, scarcely noticeable at times, monstrous at others, had long since been effaced and overlaid by invention and dream. Layer upon layer of thoughts about what hadn't been but might exist on top of the memory of what had been but might not have been. And each new layer was not merely as plausible as the one before but even more so. So what can I, what should I, remember now? What I had been asked? What

I had answered? Had I even been there at all? What about Sinevusov? Well, we can at least assume that he was there.

As were the others. They would come into Sinevusov's office during the interrogations. When he greeted his visitor the major would sometimes leap to his feet and wait for permission to resettle his backside on to the soft leather of his armchair and resume his work. But more often he just gave a friendly wave and a warm, fond smile. Not only to other majors but to those with fewer stars on their shoulders (although I never saw Sinevusov in uniform) and those without any stars at all. As far as I was concerned, he always behaved properly. Even affably. And he oozed oil endlessly.

He interrogated me at length about Istemi, the relationship that had developed between Emperor Karl and President Betancourt, the history of the wars between the Khanate and the Caliphates. He questioned me about many things, and all of it interested him. His questions often surprised me. I tried not to show it. He, on the other hand, reacted animatedly to my responses, cross-questioning me and going over the same point again and again to clarify it. And he always listened very attentively. He liked watching me draw the boundaries of our countries on a school relief map. How the greasy red line – the trail of a brand new Polish marker he'd got out of a desk drawer especially for me – crawled across the map and met up with the light-blue dotted line of the European border then broke away and set off across the living territory of sovereign states. Once

Sinevusov's superior, the general, had come upon us engaged in this activity. With a mild gesture he indicated that the major, who had leaped to his feet, should return to his seat and continue the interrogation.

By then I had extended the red boundary along the border between Bulgaria and Greece and was moving northwards along the border between Bulgaria and Yugoslavia. Following its twists and turns, I slowly made my way along the Danube. The general stopped me.

'Label it right away or else it's not clear. What's this?' He tapped his finger on the four-fingered fist of the Peloponnese.

'The Caliphates.' I wrote 'UAC' between Patra and Delphi.

'And this?' The general's finger lingered on Bulgaria.

'The Khanate.'

I noticed Sinevusov glancing warily at the general. His brow glistened with fine drops of oil.

'Write it down then!' demanded the general.

He had learned this phrase well during his years of service. I carefully traced 'ZK' on the border between Bulgaria and Romania and then, without waiting for further questions, I wrote 'SRC' on the territory of Yugoslavia and said, 'That's the Slovenorussian Confederation.'

'A bourgeois republic. Territory, 9.5 million square kilometres. Population, 210 million. Army of two million. Nuclear weapons capability,' Sinevusov briefed him.

I hadn't told him this, and he hadn't asked me. Which meant that he had found it in the documents. Or else Kurochkin had said something. For he was somewhere getting interrogated, too. Perhaps just on the other side of the wall in the next room. At the time I don't think I realized they had also arrested the other members of our group. But it wasn't hard to figure out.

The general, standing and leaning heavily on Sinevusov's desk, was examining the map carefully.

'Carry on,' he ordered.

From the Danube the Khanate's border ran northeast, dividing Romania in half and divesting Ukraine of nine of its western provinces before coming up against the blue border line. The map was finished.

Without waiting for the general to prompt me I found the right place on the map, put down a greasy dot, wrote 'Uman' in big letters and underlined it.

'The capital,' I said.

'OK, but what about the south? Who does this belong to?' He tapped on the Sea of Marmara.

'Ah, yes,' I remembered. 'It's ours.' And I partitioned the north-west from Turkey. The red stripe linked the estuaries of the Gediz, Porsuk and Sakarya rivers.

'Ours?' The general smirked. 'Do the Turks agree with that?'

'There are no Turks here. This is the ceasefire line set by the 1975 armistice. It's actually the border between the Khanate and the Caliphates. It's true that Slovenorussia thinks the straits should belong to them, but their claim isn't serious.'

'Not serious?' The general smirked again. 'Very well. Carry on.' He nodded to Sinevusov and went to the door, then stopped abruptly and asked, 'What if

Slovenorussia invades the Caliphates? Could that happen?'

'Could the Soviet Union invade Iran?' I said it to show him what rubbish he was talking. But that's not how he understood me. Everything I said they interpreted in their own way.

'What gave you that idea?' The general looked at Sinevusov, who shook his head helplessly. 'Does that mean your Slovenorussia is analogous to the Soviet Union? Is that what you mean?'

If someone wants to hear something that's what he'll hear, no matter what you say to him. All I could do was shrug my shoulders. 'If I wanted to say that I would have said it. Slovenorussia isn't the Soviet Union, and the Zaporozhian Khanate isn't . . .' I stopped and tried to think of a suitable state. 'This country has no pre-existing value,' I said, slipping in a bit of maths analysis.

At the next interrogation I drew another map for Sinevusov, this time of the Caliphates.

'Tell me,' he said, looking over the drawing, 'how did you ever come up with such a strange game in the first place?'

Sinevusov asked me this question no less than five times a day. Every day. He would choose his moment, distract me, manoeuvre like Suvorov preparing to storm the impregnable fortress of Ismail, and over and again make me repeat my answer – one short sentence that he refused to believe. I had memorized this harmless fabrication – forgive me, testimony – and recited it the way children recite Pushkin's 'Frost and

Sunshine', the way students recite the definition of material according to Lenin, the way pensioners recite the price of a hundred grams of butter. I had decided that once I said something I should stick to my story. And that's what I did. Sinevusov listened with boredom, waiting for the moment when once again, as if graced by heavenly illumination, he could marvel, 'Tell me, how did you ever come up with such a strange game in the first place?'

1983

Place names such as Apple, Little Apple, Apple Tree, Upper and Lower Apple, Greater and Lesser Apple and so forth were so common and scattered so densely throughout the province of Zhytomyr as to suggest that the most common tree in the Ukrainian north-west wasn't the oak, pine or birch but the apple tree. We drew Greater Apple for our food, bed and plunder. Three and a half weeks of *kolkhoz* life.

Like a caravan of slow black beetles, a dozen moon-lighting LAZ coaches, stiflingly hot inside, lurched off from the university student quarters at around ten thirty in the morning. One police escort with flashing lights to the front and another to the rear, our long caravan made for the west. We flew over the Kiev provincial border without even noticing. By lunchtime we were passing the town of Korostishev.

'Hey, Korostichevski,' said Nedremailo, standing in the aisle of the bus. He mispronounced Korostishevski's name so badly and so forcefully it felt like a sharp poke in the shoulder blade. 'Are we passing through the land of your forefathers?'

Sashka Korostishevski drew aside the dusty curtain and looked out the window. Stretched along the road were shrubs, short little conifers and a herd of wiry cows huddled on the verge and following us with hungry eyes.

Nedremailo paused for a moment then headed off without waiting for an answer.

Vadik Kanyuka, sitting next to Sashka, gave him a shove and said, 'He wants to swap homelands with you.'

'What for?' asked Sashka. Outside the window the shrubs had given way to enormous heaps of rubbish.

'Not that,' said Vadik irritably. Sashka wasn't taking the bait. 'What are you looking at out there?'

'I've never been here before,' Sashka drawled. 'It's interesting.'

'Prince Korostishevski makes a ceremonial entrance into the paternal appanage,' mocked Kanyuka. 'Cue the pealing of bells, the procession of the cross. Countrymen and countrywomen, shepherds and shepherdesses, old men and old women. The kissing of hands and of feet in stirrups, the right to veto the *veche* and the right to the first night on the first night . . .'

'That would be all right,' said Korostishevski. 'A principality of one's own without any maths analysis or differential equations.'

Kurochkin and I were quietly playing cards, a game of Preference. Korostishevski and Kanyuka were sitting in front of us, and we could hear their conversation.

'Think big, Korostishevski,' said Kurochkin without looking away from his cards. 'The days of petty feudal fiefdoms are long gone. Why not conquer a few

34

neighbours, unite them under your iron fist and threaten the Swedes?'

'And you're under threat, too, pal,' said Kanyuka coolly. 'You're about to take another trick when you've declared misère. Keep up now. Matters of state are being decided without you. Not just any old cook is capable of running a feudal principality, despite what Lenin said.'

The caravan of buses travelled almost as far as Zhytomyr without stopping or other hold-ups, ticking away the kilometres of the M-17 in orderly fashion. The two buses directly in front of us were the first to break away from the caravan. They turned south for Berdychiv. Soon it was our bus's turn, and blinking its lights in farewell it headed north off the M-17. Somewhere beyond Chernyakhiv, on the border of the Volodar-Volyn district, lay Greater Apple.

Dusk had fallen by the time we found the village, so it was the next day when we had a look around. It was small, its main street swimming in autumnal mud. Apple orchards circled it to the east and west, and its northern end led to the banks of the mighty Siberian-European 'River' Druzhba – oil pipeline of friendship – and just beyond the pipeline began pine forest. But we hadn't been brought to this backwoods to pump oil. We were here to pick apples – Antonovkas and Simirenkos.

And when you think about it, what else is there for radiophysics students to do in the autumn?

The village's main thoroughfare, Lenin Street, had been paved back in the 1950s and, although it was still passable, immediately beyond the village it turned into a rusty bog, by turns puddle or battered, broken road. The road went through the apple orchards, dividing them in half. On one side grew Antonovkas; on the other clusters of Simirenko. In Greater Apple everything came in twos, doubled and halved with fruity dualism. We, too, were halved, not by any particular rationale but simply into two brigades. One brigade was entrusted with Antonovkas, the other with Simirenkos. Kurochkin and I got Simirenkos.

'Reinettes are prized winter apples. What kinds of Reinette do you know?' We were being addressed by a local agronomist. Or perhaps a storekeeper or orchard manager. That is to say he was a village intellectual, wearing glasses, jacket, peaked cap and moustache (the better to hide his faint, sly smile), and he had decided to show us that we were a bunch of young louts from the capital. We were too lazy to argue with him. We were altogether too lazy.

'Now remember . . . No, you'd better write it down. Reinettes include the Baumann, Canadian, Cassel, Champagne, English, Kursk golden . . .'

'He's reciting them in alphabetical order,' Kurochkin whispered into my ear. 'He must have memorized them his first year in college and won't skip a single letter.'

'Look,' I said. 'He's counting them off on his fingers behind his back. So that he won't forget.'

'Landsberg, Orleans – that's your red saffron – paper – same as Champagne – Pisguda, *sery* – or grey – and . . .' here the gardener made a fist 'and the Simirenko.'

Then, behind his back, he stuck out an index finger and began brooding. Something was wrong.

'And the Simirenko', he repeated, 'is before you.'

Politely Mishka Reingarten reminded the gardener that he had forgotten about the Bergamot. Mishka said, 'The Bergamot Reinette was invented by Michurin who grafted the bud of an Antonovka seedling to a pear. It's medium in size, rounded and has a long storage life.'

'I give him a C,' pronounced Kurochkin, sentencing the gardener mercilessly.

'Correct,' said the gardener. 'The Bergamot. In all there are twelve varieties of Reinette.' Then, for some reason, he made a victory sign above his head. 'How did you know that?' he asked Mishka.

'Research,' said Mishka firmly.

'How did you know that?' asked Kurochkin an hour later. Mishka smirked craftily. Mishka often smirked craftily. He was working on a GTE – Global Theory of Everything. Einstein's theory of relativity fitted within the GTE as a special case. To stop the other students on the course and the residents of the dormitory from disturbing him Mishka worked on his GTE at night. And, so that he would not disturb them, he worked in a cupboard. He would put on a hooded anorak, grab a fat all-purpose notebook with dividers and a reading lamp that he secured to his neck and would spend hours at a stretch in his cupboard. He slept during the day, and he didn't go to classes at all.

'Have you ever opened up *The Great Soviet Encyclo - paedia*?' Mishka asked Kurochkin.

'I suppose so.'

'At the letter K?'

'Why would I do that?' Kurochkin didn't get it.

'Have you never even looked up your own last name?'

'I don't know – maybe. Kurochkins are as common as muck.'

'Maybe so. But Reingartens are few and far between. So I was flipping through the encyclopaedia looking for other Reingartens –'

'Misha,' Kurochkin said politely, 'I'm talking about apples.'

Mishka sighed heavily. 'Use your head, Kurochkin. "Reingarten" and "Reinette" are on the same page of the encyclopaedia. *Comprenez-vous*?'

'*Oui*,' said Kurochkin.

Kanyuka and Korostishevski had been assigned to the Antonovs. I saw them being lectured by another moustachioed gardener about Antonovkas. He also kept his hands behind his back and carefully counted on his fingers. What he was counting I don't know. Natasha Belokrinitskaya ended up with the Antonovkas. Kurochkin and I acted like nothing had happened.

* * *

Greater Apple was a two-party village. Antonovs picked Antonovkas – which they moistened and sent to the confectionery factory in Zhytomyr – and they ate apple-flavoured jelly and pastilles. They were proud that their apple was the people's choice. The Antonovs worked the orchard in three brigades called 'Antonov the Aviation Builder', 'Maksim Antonovich the Democrat', and 'Antonov-Ovseenko the Unlawfully Repressed'. The Antonovs always nominated their own candidate for chairman and intrigued in every conceivable way against the Simirenkovs. This included filing complaints against the Simirenkovs with the district and regional committees of the Party. The Antonovs thought the student brigade might call itself 'Fyodor Antonov the Artist', but our ladies reacted with unexpected alacrity, shooting down the artist and giving their brigade the highly original name of 'Antonovka'. Touched, the Antonovs appointed Kanyuka as brigadier.

But the Simirenkovs were also serious. Over the past forty years they had given the Antonovs just as good as they got and would offered no quarter in future either. They, too, always had their own candidate for chairman and their own people in the district and the region. Simirenko Reinettes from Greater Apple were sold all over the Soviet Union – from Murmansk in the north all the way to Nakhodka on the Sea of Japan. There was a cock-and-bull story going around Greater Apple that before Khrushchev opted for corn, he had been ready to plant Simirenkos the length and breadth of the country – apparently he had loved them since child-hood. But then the Antonovs had sent a courier to Moscow to tell Nikita Sergeyevich that certainly the Simirenko is a good apple, but it can't withstand mange. They recommended the Antonovka. It was the same old story – the Antonovka was the people's choice. Nikita

Sergeyevich could not have cared less – ever since Lysenko's day he'd had his fill of Antonovs – so he dashed off a few lines of invective verse to the gardeners and flew to America. But, as history tells us, he came back a changed man and decided to plant corn. Evidently it was all the same to him what the country grew. And there had been the Americans with their corn. So much for the people's apple and Lysenko.

The Simirenkovs also worked in three brigades: 'Lev Simirenko' (the vigilant instructors from the regional committee forbade 'Levok Platonovych'), 'Platon Simirenko' (publisher of the 1860 edition of Taras Shevchenko's *The Bard*) and 'Vladimir Simirenko the Repressed' (the son of Levok Platonovych, first director of the Institute of Pomology). They were ready to find a fourth Simirenko and a fifth for our brigade, but we were planning to make do with the humble name of Reinette. The Simirenkovs were aggrieved by our lack of discrimination – it scarcely mattered to us which of their precious Reinettes we chose. In order to please them without losing face, we compromised and called ourselves 'Reinette – S'. The S was a capital letter, never *ever* to be written lower-case s, so that, God willing, it wouldn't be confused with the *sery* variety . . . Kurochkin headed up the brigade, and its general management fell to Associate Professor Nedremailo.

At long last assigned to brigades, the brigades given names and schedules drawn up for kitchen duties and visits to the bath house, we were launched into battle against the harvest of this rose-family fruit tree . . . or that is what ought to have happened, but they were in no hurry to let us loose on the apples. Now it was time for theory. After all, how can you pick apples without knowing how to lay a garden, graft and regraft, properly keep cuttings in winter and shape the crown of a fruit tree? Drawings of seedlings crowded the blackboard along with examples of the right and wrong way to plant and how to prepare the garden for winter. Quotations from Columella on yellowing cardboard signs were stuck to the classroom walls.

The time passed. They fed us, let us bathe once a week and showed us a film every other day. But they wouldn't let us at the apples. The rains passed, and it was the middle of September, a warm and golden time of year. I regarded the treetops and rooftops of Greater Apple with longing, unable to comprehend what the problem was.

Not that I was itching to get into the orchard and fill wooden crates with apples. But there ought to be a reason for everything. Here I couldn't see it.

As it turned out, there was a reason. In Greater Apple Antonovkas were harvested in late August and Simirenkos in early October. They needed students in August and in October. Two applications went out to the district. The district replied that they would send students only once, either in August or October. Take your pick. But it was impossible for Greater Apple to pick one or the other – the interests of the Antonovs were blocked mercilessly by the Simirenkovs, and any proposal made by the Simirenkovs was taken by the

Antonovs as a personal slight. Yet Greater Apple couldn't refuse the students. If they refused them once, next time they wouldn't be offered at all. Which is how we ended up there in September. So as not to upset the Antonovs nor wound the Simirenkovs. But in September there was no work for us in the orchard.

When I heard this story in all its marvellous simplicity I grasped why the village didn't have a small canning facility of its own, and why – at the loss of time, money, and face – the apples were still being shipped to Zhytomyr the same way as forty years before.

It doesn't matter where I learned this, and I can't remember anyway. On the other hand, I distinctly remember how one day in class, languishing from boredom and inactivity, Kurochkin sent Korostishevski a message via pneumatic tube.

Dearest Prince Korostishevski of Zhytomyr and Volodar-Volyn, Magistrate of People's Pomology

It has come to our attention that even now the Principality of Korostishev has not mastered the daubing of branches with garden pitch or oil-based paint after pruning. It has also come to our attention that even now you have not yet been trained in the summer topping of trees. We, Princes Kurozhski, Belozhski and Krasnozhski, are prepared, at absolutely no cost to you, to distribute our new technologies throughout your backward principality. In so far as you clean your guns with bricks to this day, we shall entrust the training of your gardeners to a battalion of

Kurozhski sharpshooters. For bricks, please contact our manufacturer, Kur & Co. Home Building Supplies.

Korostishevski read the note and vanished. A reply came in the evening. Not from Korostishevski but Kanyuka.

The Order of Teutonic Orchard Lovers wishes to know more about the new garden-trimming techniques in widespread use in the Kurozh Principality. The Order's delegation of 900 knights and 5,000 armoured infantry are packing their suitcases. We propose a rendezvous and exchange of knowledge and experience on the banks of the Antonovka River. Please accept the chivalrous respects of the Grand Master of the Order KNK.

PS – Prince Korostishevski sends a brotherly kick up the arse and is detailing 800 horsemen and seven siege towers to the conference.

'You're an aggressor,' I said to Kurochkin once I had read Kanyuka's letter. 'So how are you going to reply?'

'What's to stop me saying I'll meet them with tactical nuclear weapons?'

'And how is the Kurozh Principality going to get hold of nuclear weapons?'

'How are their knights going to get hold of suit-cases?'

'They're having their little joke.'

'Well, so am I.'

'No,' I said, 'it's not the same thing.'

Kurochkin shrugged. 'Well, I like it.'

'I'd better write them myself or you'll spoil it all.'
And I wrote:

> The Zaporozhian Brothers, along with their allies the
> Tartars, Bulgars, Magyars and Khazars – countless in
> their numbers for no one has ever counted them –
> propose to meet Princes Korostishevski and Kurozhski
> and the Grand Order of Teutonic Garden Lovers for a
> friendly discussion of the urgent issues of pedigreed
> gardening. Potatoes, herring and tea to be furnished by
> your Zaporozhian hosts. Do not bother showing your
> face without horilka and mead.
>
> At your service
> Khan of the Zaporozhian Encampment, Davidov

That evening we drew up the Greater Apple Accord
and divvied up everything that could be divvied up.
Korostishevski claimed Western Europe; Kanyuka took
Asia; Kurochkin, Russia; and I fancied the rather
barbarous title Khan of the Encampment of Zaporozhye.
Then we concluded several further agreements. We
applied a common algorithm to determine army size,
population growth and technological development.
Later on I discovered that the game of Civilization is very
similar. But how could we have been playing Civilization
in Greater Apple in 1983? We were just playing a game.
There was nothing else to do. You can't just drink vodka
all the time. It gets boring.

There were four of us, which made voting awkward.

We kept coming to an impasse, two against two. We called in Reingarten for a fifth. Not so much for the game as for an uneven vote. Mishka took Mongolia, named Abakan his capital, dubbed himself Lama Undur Gegen and issued a decree that all of Mongolia should plunge itself into a state of nirvana.

* * *

'Tell me, Alex,' he would begin, gripping my wrist in a show of urgency, 'how did you ever come up with such a strange game in the first place? Where did it all come from? Where did you find all these emperors, khans, caliphates? You're Soviet students. You're at university in the capital. Who gave you the idea? Go ahead and tell me everything you know. Don't be afraid. You know you can be straight with me. We're not going to hurt you.'

What did he want me to say? 'Where did we get the idea? Someone planted it, Citizen Boss. Your secret agent and informer of many years' standing, Associate Professor Nedremailo.' Was that it? And what about the rest of them?

'Do you remember *The Black Book and Shwam - braniya*? That's where we got the idea. Lev Kassil . . .'

'Of course,' nodded Sinevusov. 'So you've said.'

I said this to him every day. No less than five times a day.

* * *

45

We were leaving Greater Apple – faces well fed, in fine health and with horticultural theory tucked under our belts – but we hadn't picked a single fruit. September was drawing to a close, and the rains were beginning. And the denizens of Greater Apple were making ready for the advance on the Simirenkos.

* * *

A dull sugary syrup; a cloudy, cloying swill; a sweet dross like that bottled and sold by my current employer – that's what my memory now dredges up. As different from what really happened as a glass of brown cola named for an apple is different from the apple itself – from the firm, fragrant, fresh apple, its yellow skin shot through with red. This Greater Apple tale harboured masses of nuances, inconsequential subtleties only just perceptible and all but indescribable. It was chock full of details that were insignificant but no less vivid for that. Such as the cottages we stayed in. We didn't stay in a school or together in a dormitory where we would have been supervised but scattered around the village. Antonovs with Antonovs, Simirenkovs with Simirenkovs. Kuroch-kin and I got a big room and an old man in a green velvet tunic as our host. I think his name was Petro. He had a wife and children long grown-up whom he regarded with such contmept that they just tried to ignore him. Which wasn't easy. Petro loafed around the village for days on end in a pair of ossified trousers, a Tyrolean hat so soiled it shone and the green velvet tunic with a pipe in the breast pocket. In the evening we played him at Preference for kopecks while drinking something vile and guffawing at his tall stories. His distant pre-Apple past crept repeatedly into his views and observations. Although his past was his own business. We only listened to the old man and didn't try to catch him out. Why ruin a good story? A little later, after the Greater Apple Accord had been signed, the countries parcelled out and the game under way, Korostishevski and Kanyuka started dropping by. They were Antonovs. Petro didn't like Antonovs. And he took a dislike to Korostishevski and Kanyuka. Kanyuka interfered in his yarns – clarifying, correcting, asking questions big and small. Just to show what was obvious. The thoroughly embittered Petro managed to sit them down for a game of Preference and stripped them of their shirts – Korostishevski lost seven roubles, and the impudent Kanyuka lost nearly fifteen, all he had. Petro cheated, that was clear, but how he did it we couldn't figure out. Of all of his children only his youngest daughter didn't sneer and turn away when he came into the house. She spent the evenings with him in our room, listening to his fables and silently watching Mishka Reingarten. She watched Mishka, and Mishka, like the rest of us, watched Natasha Belokrinitskaya. Was I really supposed to tell Sinevusov about Natasha? How much a trifling, fleeting morning conversation with her meant to each of us, and her attention, and her indifference? Surely without Natasha there never would have been a game. Rather, the game would have ended in Greater Apple. There, that's enough about Greater Apple, or I'll never finish the story.

1984

'So when did you figure out they were playing along?'

'Almost immediately. We'd explained the rules –'

'And they got interested?'

'Sure. What else were they going to do? Interrogate us? Bang on for two months about the same thing? They understood perfectly well without our help. I mean, really, was someone suddenly going to blurt out that he got the rules to the game from a cousin who'd moved to Boston five years ago? Just as an example.'

'No one could have said that.'

'I said it was just an example. That would have given them something to root around in. But as it was . . . Well, I suppose they could have manufactured a trail leading to the Mossad and given us mind-altering drugs so we'd have told them any old crap . . . only they didn't want to.'

They let us go at the end of May. Already the lilacs were in bloom and the chestnuts had nearly finished flowering. It was a lush Kiev summer. Kurochkin and I sat on Castle Hill, the oldest of the hills overlooking the Dnieper. In the authoritative opinion of the academic Peter Tolochko, this is where it had all begun – Olga, Vladimir, Yaroslav, Yuri Dolgoruki, Muscovy and the

Tsardom of Muscovy, Russia and the Soviet Union – although the cautious Tolochko did not look as far ahead as the present day. He contented himself with Vladimir and Yaroslav.

We were sitting in the high grass of Castle Hill. The sky above us, not yet leached of colour by the summer heat, was like a weightless sail full of wind; while down below bulldozers were excavating the ancient potters' and tanners' district of Gonchari-Kozhumyaki, turning entire streets into heaps of broken brick. Some of the brick and debris was carted away, the rest simply mashed into the boggy, shaky soil of the historical terrain, adding yet another cultural layer. Whatever the culture, there was the layer. But at the time we weren't up to Gonchari-Kozhumyaki. We'd been set free exactly the way we had been arrested – suddenly and unexpectedly. It was all we could talk about or think about. What had happened and what would happen next.

'So then, Alexander . . .' Sinevusov had begun the evening before, his forehead dry and smooth. The Bakin air conditioner drove a powerful stream of cold air into Sinevusov's office. 'Don't you think you've outstayed your welcome?'

He'd been calling me Alex for a long time, but he slipped in an Alexander now to emphasize the importance of the moment. I shrugged. 'You know better than I do.'

'Ho-ho,' he chortled in agreement and pointed up at the ceiling. 'We can see everything upstairs. Here's your pass.' He took a piece of cardboard from a folder and put it down in front of him. 'You're going home today. You'd like to go home, wouldn't you? We've had quite a few conversations with your mama. She's a lovely lady.'

'Uh-huh,' I said, nodding my head. He'd never said he was talking to my mother. There's a right bloody swine for you. 'You mean she's been here?'

'Sure she has, and more than once,' he let slip. He realized he had gone too far with his gossip and immediately steered the conversation in another direction. 'Let's get down to business. Alexander, for two whole months you and I have got to know each other quite well. We've grown close. We have nothing against you here. Go back to university, back to your studies, and make up for lost time.'

'Right. And just what am I supposed to say to the rector? "Sorry, I've been detained by the KGB for the past two months. Please record my unavoidable absence as sickness. Here's my certificate."'

For two months I had controlled myself, but suddenly I lost it. If only I'd known my mother was coming here, to this building, registering for passes and waiting hours to be admitted, begging for favours – she had probably wanted to give me some parcels. It was just like a slow fan being turned on behind my back, its propellers slowly beginning to knock, ratcheting up the rotations, flashing grey shadows. I realized acutely just how much I hated Sinevusov. Apparently he sensed something.

'Alex, Alex . . . What's the matter? Everything has turned out so well. You and I have understood each other perfectly.' His brow glistened faintly with oil He wiped his brow with a handkerchief, but it only became oily again. 'You have nothing to worry about. All the right people in the chancellor's office and the rector's office have been advised. Nobody's going to ask you any awkward questions. So? Better now?'

Sinevusov poured me some water. 'Here,' he said. 'It's just your nerves.' He laughed cautiously. 'Better now? Let's finish with the formalities. And part as . . . friends.'

I don't know how I would have handled the so-called formalities if he hadn't made me so angry. I really don't. Maybe I would have signed whatever he wanted me to sign. If it had got me out of that office, that building, never to return to the damp, hollow silence of its cells. Maybe we really would have parted as 'friends'. And met up from time to time – he would have asked me certain questions, and I probably would have answered those questions. Once you say 'A', you spend the rest of your life saying 'B'. I don't know what I would have done if we'd parted company as 'friends'. But already the invisible fan behind my back was driving the long grey shadows along the office wall with all its might. A glass of water wasn't enough to stop the raging machine. The shadows were running before my eyes. The fan was droning its way, officiously and mono-tonously, up to a clangour that curdled the very air in Sinevusov's office. Rotation upon rotation it pumped out fury. How do you measure fury? In atmospheres? In pascals? In millimetres of mercury?

He warned me that we were forbidden from playing our game, and should we come across any documents not turned up in the course of the search I must pass them to 33 Volodymyr Street. And to hold my tongue, not talk. I was released the same day. But we did not remain friends. This soon became obvious – and not only to me.

At the same time Kanyuka and Korostishevski got out and Kurochkin and Reingarten. Later on we found an auditorium on the fourth floor of our department and got together to talk. There was a lot to talk about. Although Kurochkin and I had met up immediately, just as soon as we could, without waiting for the others. It was literally the next day. Pallid and plumped up on government grub – they didn't stint on the portions they brought us from the cafeteria – we lay on Castle Hill in grass already grown high, succulent still and green and unmown. We warmed ourselves in the sun and looked out at Old Kiev Hill, where, according to the academic Tolochko, ancient Kiev had spread from Castle Hill (and not vice versa) sometime in the eighth century. And talked about this and that.

* * *

'It was only the first two weeks.'

'I thought it was longer.'

'No, really, it was only the first two weeks that they were serious. By then they could see there was nothing going on. Actually they knew before then. They were just making sure . . . Ryskalov was straight with me.'

I had Sinevusov; Kurochkin had Ryskalov.

'Great. You mean they just wanted to play?'

'Of course. Otherwise they wouldn't have held on to us for two months. Their usual is two weeks. They toy around with you for fifteen days, and then if it's not serious they just give you a kick up the arse and off you go.' Kurochkin made it sound macho somehow: 'toy around' and 'kick up the arse'. From the heights of Castle Hill our late prison didn't look quite real. A bit sinister perhaps but not real. And already just a little bit forgotten.

'Couldn't they have managed without us? I mean, the rules are easy enough. A schoolboy could learn them in a couple of hours.'

'Sure they could have,' Kurochkin laughed merrily. 'But they're not schoolboys. They're secret police, dogs of sovereigns. They're at work, getting paid by the state. It wasn't for the game, not the way you understand it. They thought: Hey let's play with them. And sent a report upstairs: "Everything is under control. We're conducting a counter-intrigue. We're investigating the specifics, getting into character."'

I remembered how Sinevusov kept nudging my arm at first. 'Alex,' he said, 'come on, let's get them. We've got a bomb, so let's get them. It'll be too late when they've made a bomb of their own. The time is right.'

Sinevusov always wanted to fight Ryskalov. They were friends. Kind of like Kurochkin and me.

'They'd better return Itil,' said Sinevusov, who was trying to wear me down. 'I mean, it's our ancient capital, where our roots are and the graves of our ancestors. Or aren't you Russian, Alex.'

'We're Zaporozhians, Citizen Major,' I reminded him with satisfaction.

'Whatever,' he said, dismissing my comment with some irritation. 'Are we going to get them or not?'

But I ducked it. I had a strategy of my own, and it worked. I didn't fight, I traded. For example, Slovenorussia was fighting the Holy Russian Empire. I sold tanks and anti-aircraft guns to one, aeroplanes and self-propelled artillery to the other. An American tactic. I used the money I made to buy up all the plutonium on the world market and build atomic weapons. Not for sale but for me. So no one would think about getting hold of my anti-aircraft guns and aeroplanes without paying for them. Sinevusov understood soon enough that on my team he wouldn't get to fight, so instead he incited Kurochkin's and Kanyuka's interrogators to fight Korostishevski. In the past this wouldn't have been possible: Kanyuka/Caliph Al-Ali always sided with Korostishevski/Emperor Karl XX. They had signed a peace treaty. They were allies. But obviously Kanyuka's interrogator was able to pressure him. He'd found Kanyuka's Achilles' heel. The Caliphates invaded the Holy Roman Empire simultaneously in two places, beginning a war for La Mancha and Andalusia while also landing troops in Sicily. Then Kurochkin/Betancourt dispatched twenty-five tank divisions into Gorizia and Aquileia.

Our officers weren't kidding around; they were

really drawn into the game. Sinevusov sat for hours with the cards, working out alternative scenarios on his calculator. His little grey suit jacket from Kiev's Maxim Gorky clothing factory would be lying on the window ledge, his tie somewhere else – a dark-blue tie with a dash of marine, a gift from his colleagues. Sinevusov would snap his braces, sweat under his arms, wipe his brow and keep on asking, 'What would you do if they did this? And what would you do if they did that?'

I don't know how it was with Kurochkin and Ryskalov, but I was the only one playing for the Khanate. Sinevusov may have been afraid to assume personal responsibility even in a game, or maybe there was some other reason, but he only advised. And did he ever advise – obstinately, tediously and wearyingly. But the decisions were taken by me. I didn't fight. I traded. Everything with everyone. The Khanate grew rich and highly developed. However, even though I observed my customary neutrality in the war with the Holy Roman Empire, I supplied arms more willingly to Korostishevski than Kanyuka. I sold him my new anti-aircraft systems on condition that they not be used against Slovenorussia. Only against the Caliphates. Weapons trading was a confidential business, but Sinevusov was sitting there right next to me ensuring that Ryskalov and his comrades were kept up to date. There was nothing I could do about it. I helped Korostishevski however I could; it looked like they were giving him a really hard time. And not just in the game. Above all, not just in the game. But he was withstanding the blows.

And in that war, predatory and unjust, the war of the three majors, Korostishevski only lost Aquileia. That town went to Slovenorussia. Whereas Kanyuka put his people on the Iberian Peninsula in vain. He had wasted his money buying my two rocket cruisers.

* * *

Later, sitting up on Castle Hill and looking down at Kiev in May, I knew, with a distinct and vivid certainty, that our biggest problems were behind us and nothing worse would happen. Could there really be something worse than the prison inside the KGB building? Surely not. So it could only get better. There was nothing to fear. But within a week, my recent optimism abandoned me. One week later I knew that anything could happen. And that things could get even get worse.

I haven't been back up Castle Hill since then. Probably for no good reason. The view from there is marvellous. Marvellous and very precise – no aberrations, no distortions. Now, twenty years on, I can see that the hill was right and I was wrong. But what can you take from me now? I'm just a peddler of fizzy drinks. Who cares if I perish in a red-and-white peddler's tent in the cold of winter or whether in that same tent I sweat the caustic sweat of labour in the summer. I'm now a peddler of fizzy drinks, and my affairs no longer take me to Castle Hill. But back then . . . Then, Istemi was behind me, and we were equals. Not in everything, but in some ways we were. And Castle Hill knew it.

Perhaps it's only because of Istemi that I managed

to get out of the gloomy, grey-granite building on Volodymyr Street in a way that didn't cast a dark shadow over the rest of my life. It was Istemi who brought Sinevusov to heel, Istemi who refused to collaborate, Istemi whom they set free. Noses pressed against the part-open door, they observed him going out on to Volodymyr Street and standing there, renewing his acquaintance with the May sunshine and deciding which way to go – left towards Opera Street or right towards the park on Volodymyr Hill. They observed his first steps as a free man, and the oil mingled with the venom and trickled down their cheeks and from their chins. And when he reached Malopidvalna Street and disappeared from view, they carefully drew their breath and wiped away the oil and venom. They let Istemi go, and along with Istemi I left, too.

1984

In winter the university lecture halls were unbelievably cold. The windows are enormous – they take up an entire wall – and no radiator can compensate for the expansive spirit of the architects. That said, the radiators don't exactly tax themselves – they are only vaguely warm. But, when you think about it, had the architects actually done anything wrong? The buildings had been constructed to an excellent design. A design that won second place in a competition. The competition was held in Mexico. Or maybe it was Colombia. Either way, a country in the Caribbean – maybe even Cuba – had decided to build a university and organized a competition. The winner took everything, and the runner-up got Kiev. Because the powers that be in Kiev decided to take advantage of the competition to save themselves a bit of money. That was the national mentality coming through. They opted for a ready-made design and bought it for next to nothing. After all, Kiev is a well-known tropical city, which is why we have a fine time of it in winter, and summer's not bad, either. When the time came to approve the budget, the air conditioning was dispensed with. With great big windows like those, reasoned the Ministry of Education steering committee, who needs air conditioning? This is no Cuba and no Mexico either, thank God! If it gets too warm, just open a window. Look how big they are.

Down below, the cracked base of a dried-up fountain was turning grey. We weren't about to open the window, even though we had barred the door closed with a mop. Term was in full throttle, testing drawing to a close and exams just beginning. We had to do something while we could.

This was no Congress of Victors. Although there had been a victory of sorts – we had got out. Each of us had encountered freedom in the place prescribed in the manual – at the entrance, alongside the officer on duty. Or at the exit, rather. The interrogations were in the past. The hollow silence of the corridors and cells of the KGB prison had dissipated. And there had been a victory. But it had not turned us into victors.

Kanyuka was sitting by the window, looking out at the golden scene beyond without actually seeing it, occasionally drumming a nervous tattoo on the back of the next desk. Korostishevski was bobbing his leg up and down, attentively studying his old trainers. His lips were outthrust, and he was humming something indistinctly. They didn't look at one another, didn't see one another and didn't want to. The war of the three majors was long over and in the past, and Kurochkin had got Aquileia. But it wasn't the unconscionable capture of a small seaside town that distressed Korostishevski; it was Kanyuka's perfidious aggression that he couldn't forgive.

'What's his problem? I didn't attack him. Can't he

see?' said Kanyuka in loud indignation, turning first to me, then Kurochkin. 'It wasn't me. I was only doing as I was told. They said, "Do it", and I did it. If you want we can start the game over again. Tell him, all of you, tell him it's not too late to start over if he wants to. Can't we?'

'He' – Korostishevski, studying a crack he had noticed in the sole of one of his trainers – shook his head in disappointment and hummed a wordless tune.

'It wasn't me, make him understand,' Kanyuka demanded of Kurochkin. 'You were fighting him your-self.'

Kurochkin paced alongside the blackboard, from wall to window and back again. He didn't say anything, but I knew Kurochkin was glad. Was there actually something to be glad about? But Kurochkin was glad. Although he didn't show it as he paced, frowning, from window to wall and back again.

'Let's assume we can't start over,' replied Kurochkin at last. 'And we won't. You're an adult Vadik. You've reached your legal majority, so you have to take responsi - bility for your actions – or at least you should. They were only telling you what you *should* do, but you yourself decided.'

'Me?' Kanyuka jumped up and ran along the row of desks. 'Ha! So it was me deciding, was it?'

I couldn't stop myself saying, 'Can't the two of you sort this out between yourselves later on? We're not here to negotiate a peace treaty or clarify who attacked whom and why. We've got to finish the term. And agree a separate exam schedule with the rector's office. There's not just one or two of us, but five – we're almost a group. Or else we need to go on academic leave immediately. Right?'

Kanyuka looked out the window again. Korostishevski bobbed his leg. Kurochkin paced silently along the blackboard.

'Whether or not we take our exams, or whether or not we can come to some agreement,' came the voice of Mishka Reingarten, who was gazing at the wall, 'what's that compared with the diamond path of the Buddha? Against the practice of *phowa*? And what value does life have before death anyway? We must learn how to transform our consciousness into a state of beatitude. At the moment of dying.'

'What's that mean – at the moment of dying?' asked Korostishevski.

'It means,' said Kanyuka, who no one had asked, 'pulling out your intestines and studying them. And if it doesn't work the first time, you quickly put them back and start over again.'

'Why don't we discuss the business at hand?' I said. They were beginning to annoy me. 'Who's going to see the rector?'

'We can't afford to lose this year,' agreed Kanyuka gloomily. 'Otherwise it's the army.'

Kurochkin shrugged. 'If it's got to be the army, then so be it. We'll fight. If not, then it's exams. We'll take them.'

'In other words, we'll take our exams. End of.'

Kanyuka wanted to have the last word. But on the last word – 'of' – his voice broke into an almighty squeak and he started coughing.

'I'll be back,' I said. I pushed the mop aside and went out into the corridor. They might go on like that for a while yet. I decided to find out whether they would see us in the rector's office. Either the rector, if he was in, or the assistant rector. But no one was there. This was very unusual during exams. It was hot and deserted. An infernal silence had fallen upon the entire floor around the rector's office. A dry, withered silence that buzzed in my ears and ached in the back of my neck. There was only a secretary working at fever pitch. On the other side of the wall, in a furious and unhealthy frenzy, she was hammering away on the keys of a Yatran typewriter. I began reading the notices posted around the door, timetables, instructions, orders: '. . . allow students to take examinations on the condition that . . .'; '. . . do not allow in the event that . . .' It was like a dream where suddenly you know what must happen next. I was alone in the corridor when the percussive Yatran came to a stop, and the silence grew deafening and unbearable. The secretary came out of the office, and, not paying me any attention, amid the old notices she pinned up yet another, a new one. At that very moment footsteps became audible from the far end of the corridor. I turned and looked. Slowly passing the doors to the lecture halls and displays of dusty book covers and the yellowed title pages of academic articles approached Natasha Belokrinitskaya. I don't remember where the secretary went – I was waiting for Natasha – and only later did my eyes fall upon the short paragraph of text. It was an order from the rector regarding our expulsion.

'It's so economically worded,' said Kanyuka five minutes later with false admiration. '"For the systematic violation of academic discipline" – you can't argue with that.'

They were examining the sheet of paper I had taken down from the departmental notice board, turning it over in their hands and passing it along to one another. The sheet, which had been clean and white a moment before, grew creased as it passed from hand to hand. It was deteriorating before our very eyes, and yet it was full of power – even now we could scarcely hold it. We had been expelled.

Natasha was standing by the board and watching us silently. She was watching us, and we were all trying to understand which one. And what she was thinking about. What exactly. She was watching, and Korosti-shevski and Kanyuka were both trying to look cheerful and carefree. Kurochkin frowned pensively and rested his cheek on his fist. Mishka Reingarten attempted to speak.

'Well, sure,' he said to Kanyuka, 'we've been truant for two months. Do we have doctor's certificates? No. That means we've been truant. We're being expelled for truancy.'

'We weren't truant. We were in gaol. Although, now you mention it, perhaps we could get certificates? I hear the KGB issues them.'

'Volodymyr Street?' asked Kurochkin with surprise. 'Certificates? Who told you that?'

'I'm not sure,' said Kanyuka in some confusion. 'I just heard it somewhere.'

'You should try to remember where,' advised Kurochkin warmly.

'That's enough,' said Sashka Korostishevski softly, and they fell silent. We could see it all. We were being expelled, but at least it was only for truancy. They didn't want to make a big deal of it – call meetings, expel us from the Komsomol. They could if they wanted to. But they were expelling us gently – and that was well and good. It left us the possibility of studying elsewhere. It could have been worse.

2004

Kurochkin's secretary caused a commotion in the office and just about disrupted an Important Meeting. When he couldn't get hold of me on my mobile (we're under orders to keep our mobiles switched off when we discuss that holiest of holies – 'milk yields', better known as 'revenue'), he started dialling the bosses. 'Davidov is in a meeting,' said our patient office managers to Kuroch - kin's persistent secretary. 'You can leave a message if you want to.'

'I'm calling from Parliament – the Finance and Banking Committee. Davidov is being summoned as a matter of urgency to a meeting of the committee.' 'Summoned as a matter of urgency' did the trick. Maybe our office is American, but the managers are local. They know better than to deal with the authorities if at all possible and immediately passed responsibility to the brass. They told Malkin.

Stephen Malkin was top dog at our branch. He had returned the night before from Memphis, Tennessee, where there had been a great pow-wow of regional managers at our fizzy giant's head office. The head honchos were explaining the party line on *per capita* 'milk yields'. As far as I could see, nothing had changed – it was still all about profit. But it was necessary to expound on the topic at least once a quarter in case we forgot. Malkin had brought back a box of DVDs of the Memphis meeting and gave one to each of us. Now he was doing his best to convey the chief's exhortations to consider night and day whether we were doing everything we could for the good of the company. Malkin talked, and we took notes – or, in truth, pretended to, and it was inhumanly boring at that.

Every time I attended one of these meetings I recalled with a shudder of nostalgia my army political indoctrination of eighteen years before. Twice a week we were assembled by battery commander Major Razin, who dictated at length from a Party-approved training manual. The battery commander was short in stature, with two dozen iron teeth gleaming darkly from his mouth. He himself was a die-hard Stalinist. Whenever he came across the leader's name within the approved text he grew inordinately excited and forgot all about the training manual and the political classes. 'We couldn't have done it without Joseph,' he cried exultantly. 'Wherever you look – there he is. We'd have got nowhere without him. That's because he was the head – he and he alone thought for everyone else, for the entire country. Not long ago our pay went up. That's good, isn't it? Don't you think they did the right thing? Well, what do you suppose Joseph did? He lowered the prices. One's as long as the other is broad, eh? But if you look closely . . . when they raise wages, we pay more taxes. But what about prices? Eh? Eh? That's right. Because he was looking after the people.' We loved these monologues – they revealed the weakness of a strong man, and we thought of the battery commander as a strong man. Then we just took it easy. There was no need to take notes on these monologues. And Stalin was the last thing on our minds.

Malkin was nothing like Razin. He looked like a hamburger: plump buns, spirit of democracy, big smile on display. In his callow American youth Malkin had studied at the same college as William F. Hume, president of the board of directors of our little shop, so whenever when he came across the name Hume in those management documents that showered on us like incessant rain from Memphis, Tennessee, Malkin would get as excited as Major Razin. He would completely forget about the documents and volubly hold forth about that down-to-earth American guy, Bill As He Remembered Him. We didn't hold it against Malkin. Without this chatter Important Meetings would have been a lot harder to bear. I don't know what the others were thinking while they listened to Malkin, but I had long since stopped listening altogether. I would look at Malkin and wait – for the moment his synthetic smile gave way to a Razinesque iron grin and those immortal words would resound: 'That's because he was the head – he and he alone thought for everyone else.'

On this occasion Malkin was shot down before he gained altitude. His eyes had not yet misted over, his voice had yet to quiver in pride and excitement. He had only managed a solemn recitation of the signature on a management directive when one of the office managers slunk into the room like a silent shade trying not to detach itself from the wall. Malkin twitched, smiled broadly and – burying his irritation deep inside – eyed the manager, who redoubled his pace to cross the room and bend over the chief's ear. Malkin heard the fellow out. For a moment his brows vaulted indignantly then smoothed out again, and Malkin assumed a stock smile. He gave a curt nod and a rapid reply. I was allowed to go.

A minute later I was talking to Kurochkin on the telephone, and within fifteen minutes I was turning off Three Saints Boulevard on to Kostel Street where he lived. Rush hour was starting, and the city centre was packed with cars, but I was able to avoid the worst of it by taking quiet back streets. If I'd gone by Volodymyr Street or Kreschatik Boulevard it would have taken me until evening.

Kurochkin was standing in the doorway to his living-room. 'Comprador,' I said, 'what have you brought this country to? There are so many cars in the city you can hardly shove your way through them. If people keep growing poor at this rate, we'll need double-decker roads.'

'And a car park instead of the Monastery of the Caves.'

'There's not much room there.'

'We'll expand it, make it deeper. Install air conditioning, plumbing and electricity.'

'Nothing is sacred to you, is it, Kurochkin?' I sighed with disappointment.

'Nothing,' said Kurochkin. 'It's my habit to drink the blood of Christian babies in the morning instead of juice, and I like to nibble on the relics of the monastery's saints.'

I imagined Kurochkin in the kitchen with a glass of blood and a brown leg of Saint Nestor the Chronicler on his plate. At the very thought my stomach rebelled, and I began to gag.

'Ah, I see that's making you queasy,' Kurochkin observed, 'but I kid you not. Some guy actually has suggested modernizing the caves. I'm going to turn the scheme down tomorrow, but in a couple of days all the papers – all the papers he owns – will start smearing me with shit. Just wait and see.'

'All right,' I said vaguely, 'although you don't exactly look intimidated. Just a few days ago I read that you've been declared the Ukrainian government's sex symbol.'

'Ah. Don't read the gutter press before lunch, doctor.'

Of course you didn't have to read it – Kurochkin wouldn't look any less attractive. Around twenty years before, someone, probably Kanyuka, had called Kurochkin the 'human numeral 1'. Long and skinny, with a prominent nose, chin and Adam's apple and a stomach you could feel his spine through, he aroused the pity and compassion of every woman the wrong side of thirty. He was fed by the ladies from the lunchroom, the cleaning ladies, the mothers and grandmothers of his friends and acquaintances – and my mother especially. I seem to recall Kurochkin being remarkably omnivorous. As the years went by he grew heavier. Beneath his light artificial tan one could now detect a tender layer of flab. The former 'numeral 1' was nowhere in sight. Kurochkin was smooth and sleek, and if not for his regular bouts with iron weights he would have looked more like a 0. A lean, fit 0.

'Any more mail today?' he asked.

'Not this morning, no. Nothing important, anyway.'

'Good. You'll remember this, of course . . .'

He put a print-out of the ultimatum in front of me. 'Recent history has shown that there exists within Slovenorussia . . .'

'I remember.'

'It looks like he's done what he said he would do and started a war.'

'What do you mean *he*?'

'Who else? Sasha Korostishevski, the Holy Roman Emperor.'

That was impossible. Kurochkin knew just as well as I did that Korostishevski could not start a war. In early October 1986, when all the active-duty troops in our conscription were being demobilized by order of the Ministry of Defence of the USSR and we old-timers were hurriedly pasting the last photographs into our demob albums, Sashka's APC was ambushed outside the Afghan town of Herat and subjected to heavy fire. The tank burned up. So did Sashka and the rest of his crew. That is a fact, an absolute fact. No one was saved.

'I see. You're shadowboxing.'

'Davidov! Yesterday his shadow stripped me of 90 million. And this is just the start.'

'An impressive start,' I agreed. 'But try as you may, you won't strip me of 90 million. Why don't you tell me everything from the beginning.'

'OK,' Kurochkin nodded. 'But not now. I've got something to show you. Let's go.'

'I can just imagine. If I had any children I'd tell them never to drink my company's cola and to steer clear of your surprises.'

We stepped outside. From the soggy plywood entrance to the Roman Catholic church a priest opened his damp arms to us.

'Let's take your car,' said Kurochkin. He winced and turned up the collar of his coat. 'Mine's got about a dozen bugs in it. What dreadful weather. Three weeks into spring, and it's as cold as New Year's Day. What a country. Let's get going.'

'Where to?'

'We're going to lunch. I usually eat about now. The place isn't far from here.'

Kurochkin apparently had lunch by the Golden Gates. We could have walked there in fifteen minutes. Instead it took us nearly an hour in the car. The whole of the city centre was clogged like a blocked drain.

When I saw we were stuck and were going be stuck for some time, I said, 'You should have brought your flashing lights. You do have flashing lights, don't you?'

'What do I want flashing lights for?' he growled. 'They just annoy people pointlessly. I'm sure you've

71

blown a gasket or two when idiots with flashing lights get in your way. Why don't you have a look at this while we're waiting?' He passed me the letter.

A polite gentleman who referred to Kurochkin as 'my dearest Yuri' wrote that this year unforeseen circumstances in world markets had prevented him from entirely fulfilling agreements concluded at his ranch three years before. The gentleman hoped Yuri would show the understanding befitting a wise statesman and gave assurances of his unswerving feelings of friendship. The writer of the letter gave his name simply as Michael. No surname, no position. Just Michael.

'Is that your 90 million?' I asked Kurochkin after reading the letter twice.

He tilted his head and didn't say anything.

'What does Sashka Korostishevski have to do with it?'

'Can't you see?'

'No,' I replied honestly.

'You didn't read it carefully. What's this?' he said and pointed to a couple of letters at the bottom of the page.

'Y.T.' I read and shrugged. 'That could mean all sorts of things. It could be a printing glitch and not mean anything at all.'

'A printing glitch!' Kurochkin flared up. 'A printing glitch worth 90 million dollars, eh? It's not just YT, Davidov. No way is it just YT. Do you remember now?'

I did remember. Whenever we moved our troops, advanced or retreated, we had written 'your turn', usually just 'YT', to confirm that we'd made our final decision. How eerie those letters looked in the letter from this unknown Michael – unknown to me but evidently well known to Kurochkin. Looking at the letters I felt something in the world change for ever – some axis shifted, the stream of time changed course, even the sky abruptly changed colour. Somewhere close at hand horns began to sound impatiently.

'Hey, keep your eyes on the road.' Kurochkin brought me down to earth. 'It's almost evening on a Friday, and people are irritable. Come on, let's get going.'

To the blowing of horns and invective of other drivers gridlocked alongside us, we slowly moved forward.

'Kurochkin,' I said, 'you may be right.'

'I wish I wasn't, Alex,' Kurochkin sighed. 'You know this money doesn't belong to me. Not to me personally. These ninety lemons are gone, but another ninety must not disappear. There's no point in my telling you all the details, but you can be damn sure it's being watched. Speaking of which, can you please keep the letter confidential? It's not dangerous that you've read it, but please don't broadcast it either. Maybe the bloke who's been waiting for us the past hour at Rabelais will know what's going on.'

'What bloke?'

'I said it's a surprise.'

'Another one? I thought the letter was your surprise. And who's Michael?'

Kurochkin jerked his head. 'It doesn't matter.'

'Why not?' I asked uncomprehendingly. 'He's playing against you, and you –'

'He's not the one playing, Davidov. Can't you see that? He's just a respectable man who's been to Ukraine two or three times for all of ten hours, no more. He's never even heard of our game and doesn't know a thing about it. But somehow they've managed to make a move. Do you know what that means? Just think who it might be . . .'

I shrugged. 'I don't know,' I said indifferently. The words 'respectable man' had lost meaning for me ages ago. It was just an abstract idea. Maybe Kurochkin thought he was a respectable man, but he was a nobody. It was a long time since I had trusted anyone's judgement but my own. 'Who do you think it might be?'

Kurochkin curled his lip. 'At least we know it's not their president.'

Our people are unswerving and steadfast in their contempt from afar for figures imbued with power, and, despite his previous incarnation as Deputy Premier, Kurochkin was no different. A friend of mine came to visit a few years ago – by that time he'd been living in America for around twenty years – the television was switched on and Clinton was being broadcast live, his cheeks and neck varying in hue from deep beet-red to floury-white and back to ripe beet again. He was giving testimony on his private life, and the whole world, billions of viewers, were appreciating his chameleon-esque abilities.

'Our wonderful president . . .' my friend said knowingly

and nodded at the television with the grimace of a man who's bitten into a lemon. At that moment I recalled that in the happy days of pre-Rasputin St Petersburg the public had referred to the tsar as Our Colonel of Tsarskoe Tselo and probably pulled similar faces and winked. But as soon as such a citizen comes face to face with an important official, then for months afterwards he spouts butter and honey and contorts his spine into a studied faint bow. Even the words he uses change.

'By the way,' I said, checking myself abruptly, 'Did you notice that the letters YT are in the wrong place? They're not supposed to be in the letter itself.'

'What do you mean "not supposed to"?'

'Well, they're not in the ultimatum, for example. Remember? You could transfer several documents in one move, but YT was used . . .'

'That's right. We put YT only on memoranda that listed all the actions taken in a turn . . . No,' he interrupted himself and started laughing, 'they have done everything correctly. If the entire move consists of this one letter, then there's no need for a memorandum.'

'But how do you know this was the last action in the move?'

'They put YT where they did so that I wouldn't expect a memorandum or any other documents.'

Once I parked the car on Golden Gate Street we plunged into the March mud and made our way to Rabelais. I was overcome by a sense of unreality, of the impossibility of what was happening.

* * *

The person waiting for us in the restaurant was Sinevusov. Almost as soon as Kurochkin had mentioned a surprise, I knew there was something I didn't like. Now I knew why.

If I hadn't seen the major again twelve or thirteen years before I wouldn't have recognized him now. It had been a time of demonstrations and queues. Then we thought it appropriate to divide population into two groups: progressive and forward-thinking people like us who were demonstrating and fighting for our rights and freedoms, and people like them, the backward *silent majority*, fed at the hand of an inhumane regime, who stood in queues for vodka and liver sausage. Although the demonstrators needed vodka and liver sausage no less than those who learned about the demonstrations from the television news.

It was late autumn and already cold. I had stopped by a tea shop on Kreschatik. These days it bakes and sells incredibly delicious apricot and prune buns straight from the oven, but back then there was nowhere on all of Kreschatik where you could have a hot tea and bun. At the time the shop was offering swill of some sort and petrified-cheese sandwiches. I stood in the queue warming myself and looking around, expecting to see familiar faces. You see familiar faces all over Kiev; the more you look, the more you see. I didn't notice Sinevusov immediately. The queue was snaking its way between the little tables, and for a while the major was hidden in a bend. I didn't see him until I was nearly upon him, although I still didn't recognize him.

He had aged noticeably. His cheeks sagged, his face was grey and he had grown out what little hair he had left and gathered it into a ponytail – a dirty-grey ponytail. Before, he had looked youngish and blond – albeit blond with bald patches – and he had considered himself a blond beast.

The major was at the counter chatting with a tall, stout man in an old brown windcheater.

I overheard Sinevusov's tenor saying 'You keep going on and on about Faulkner, Faulkner . . .' His voice hadn't changed. Which is when I realized – no, realized isn't the word; I *felt* who he was, and I was badly shaken. 'Faulkner was a student of Dostoevsky who didn't finish the course. He was running around Yoknapatawpha in short trousers with a Nobel Prize medal dangling around his neck, but he was still peering out from behind his fingers at Dostoevsky . . . What? What's the matter?'

The stout man in the windcheater was muttering something quietly. Obviously he disagreed with Sinevusov.

'What sources? Forget it. The sources are all the same, trust me. And people don't have such Kara - mazovian depths either. The Karamazovs are a fiction – the creation of a brilliant writer, all three of them. What? Well, yes, of course, all four. I was, that is I . . . Look, they're demonstrating on the square. Don't you want to go see? Two hundred metres from here. I've had enough of it. Democrats. No one knows them better than me.' He took a sip of tea. Beads of oil mixed with venom oozed on his brow and upper lip. 'But, if you will, I'm the number-two democrat in this city. Everyone else was still standing at attention and reporting to the Party Congress as usual, but I –'

At this point the stout man apparently asked about the number-one democrat. Sinevusov named someone I'd never heard of before – the name meant nothing to me.

I didn't approach Sinevusov then. I had no desire to chew the fat with him about the past. We had no common past.

* * *

'Recognize him?' asked Kurochkin as we crossed the room to the table. Sinevusov had been waiting a while – we were more than an hour late.

'Thanks a lot. I've been dreaming of this meeting all my life.'

'Ho-ho!' He raised his hand and stopped. 'Don't get carried away now.'

'Whatever,' I said. 'We don't fight old men.'

Writing Sinevusov off as an old man was stretching it a little. If he had been around forty back then, he was sixty now. That didn't exactly make him old. And my major was looking great. He hadn't cut off the ponytail; on the contrary, he'd let it grow even longer. The ponytail had briskly silvered to a cold bright grey, and the folds and wrinkles on his face created a unified picture. Sinevusov had at last grown into his own face. It wasn't much, but it was his.

Lunch, or dinner as far as I was concerned, was all

business. No one showed any surprise or any particular emotion. No one said, 'It's been ages!' or 'Hasn't time flown?' or any other formulaic nonsense. We shook hands briefly, as if we'd just met the night before. That was all. Only once did I catch Sinevusov appraising me with a brief sideways glance. All evening Sinevusov said nothing. He said nothing and ate. Kurochkin spoke.

It seemed that I no longer knew Kurochkin – or, rather, I'd never got to know the Kurochkin of today. Sometimes you can just tell what kind of an adult a child will become. But back when I knew him well, when we were close, Kurochkin had been different. If you accept that a person is the sum of his experience, back then the Kurochkin of today hadn't begun to develop. He was the only one of us who managed a fresh start at university after the army. Although 'all of us' is misleading. By then we were only three of the original five: Kurochkin, Kanyuka and me. Sashka Korosti-shevski didn't come back from Afghanistan, and Mishka Reingarten was spending his third year in room 103 of the Frunze Street Hospital. Mishka had tried to evade the army on the grounds that he was a nutter, but the doctors evaluating his case determined he wasn't just a draft dodger and his ailment really did require urgent treatment. If Mishka was still alive, then they were treating him to this day. I hadn't seen him for a long time, around ten years.

After the army Kurochkin enrolled in law school and graduated. I, like an idiot, tried to re-enter the waters of our old university's radiophysics department. The waters rejected me. As for Kanyuka, he didn't even try. He earned a little money, bought a video recorder, opened a video shop in his apartment and used his brains to go into business.

In the late 1980s Kurochkin and I were still getting together regularly, but after he finished his studies he suddenly began appearing on television in the company of some rather well-known figures, and soon he himself became someone of interest to journalists. In other words, he had begun a political career. And he made it.

This was the first time I had seen Kurochkin at work – that our lunch was work was immediately apparent. Although, of course, on a ministry committee he would behave differently – that's because the FORMAT was different.

Once we'd settled around the table Kurochkin gave a succinct and matter-of-fact account of the situation. He said, 'We've been struck', followed by 'We're being set up', and 'I'm already being asked awkward questions', then 'Solve the problem and get rid of the question.'

He concluded with 'We have to find him first. Is that clear?'

Sinevusov was chewing zestfully. He didn't raise his head or look away from his plate. Everything was clear.

'I can't make head nor tail of it.' I shrugged and looked at Kurochkin. 'What kind of salad is this? It has such a surprising taste, but it's delicate, too. It's like there's citrus and fish and some Ukrainian fruit – apples, maybe. I can't figure it out. Do you know?'

Sinevusov grunted softly.

'Davidov!' Kurochkin frowned. 'Stick to business, please.'

'Of course.' I pushed my plate away. 'I'll stick to business. Number one. Yurka, what makes you think you can tell me what to do? I'm not one of your wretched ministers, and I'm not about to bow down and salute you – not for any reason.'

'OK, OK,' said Kurochkin with a sweep of his arm. 'If that's all –'

I cut him short. 'Don't interrupt me.' The hatred in my lightning outburst scorched my consciousness and whipped up the shade of Istemi from the depths. I was a little bewildered. I hadn't expected anything of the kind from myself. After all, I counted Kurochkin among my friends, and he had come to my assistance a few times in a big way. But that didn't give him the right to decide what I should or shouldn't do. 'I'm not done yet. Number two. I don't intend to go on a manhunt, and I shall not do so. There's nothing for me to do here. No money has been taken from me. Kickbacks, embezzle - ment, fraud – that's your affair. Your affair and your millions. You began without me, and you can carry on without me. If you want to fish your chestnuts out of the fire, find somebody else. I pass. And as far as the game is concerned, we finished in 1984. That's enough for me. I'm not going to start playing again. Thank you for dinner. We've finished.'

'You're missing the point, Davidov,' said Kurochkin. In his voice there was nothing but endless patience.

'Our people think – for the moment anyway – that it's the Americans. And the Americans are like the elements.' He recited a line of Pushkin. '"The storm covers the sky with gloom" – remember that? It's about them, the bread-winners. Either they're howling like animals or whining like children, but it's impossible to understand why or, more importantly, to predict what will happen tomorrow. But as soon as they do find out, and we have to be ready for this, then it won't be because of the Americans any more but because of us. I don't want to scare you, but anyone who's had anything to do with the game can expect big trouble.'

'They'll tear you to shreds,' said Sinevusov, moment-arily looking away from his plate before going straight back to his food.

'Did you hear that?' Kurochkin pointed at Sinevusov. 'They'll tear us to shreds – me first, then you – if we don't track him down.'

'If we don't track who down, Kurochkin?'

'Sashka Korostishevski. It's coming from him. Even if it has nothing to do with him, we have to track down whoever is responsible for this letter. It's our turn now, can't you see?'

'It's your turn now, Kurochkin. Yours. Not ours. Don't drag me into your affairs.'

'You're wrong, Davidov.'

'Maybe. I make lots of mistakes. Which is precisely why I don't want to add your mistakes or anyone else's to my own. I make enough all by myself. Whether or not I can help you is something else . . .'

'That's what we're talking about.'

'Helping someone isn't the same as carrying out your or someone else's orders. I'll do only what I myself consider necessary.'

'But coordinate with me.'

'Agreed. But if I don't want to do something I won't do it.'

'Agreed.'

Kurochkin gave me Sinevusov as my assistant. Or perhaps he just wanted him to keep an eye on me . . .

What kind of bloody life is that when you can't even trust your own friends?

* * *

I'd been glued to my computer screen since morning. It was displaying a complicated table with the results of cola sales in the four northern provinces of Ukraine. By now I'd memorized the contents of the table and no longer even noticed it.

I was trying to piece together a picture of some sort using the sorry fragments Kurochkin had scattered before me, and I could see nothing would come of it. The fragments were too few – I had no idea where they belonged. And it wasn't just that we – or I (I wasn't sure Kurochkin had told me everything he knew) – didn't have enough information, but the story was also short on characters. The light in the auditorium was switched off, the show had begun and was well under way, but they had forgotten to turn on the spotlights. Or didn't want to. Perhaps that was part of the concept. The director, a bloody avant-gardist, had staged a show without lights. The action develops, it twists and turns, and from the set you hear, 'She loves him but not like a husband. It's a childhood friendship.' A meaningful-poisonous-sceptical response follows. 'We know this friendship. If only there wasn't . . . an obstacle.' Pause. The creak of a door, a bang, and the voice again, 'What are you doing?' We're meant to guess that the chamber-maid has entered the room. We're meant to guess what the chambermaid looks like and who Anna Pavlovna is and who's playing Sasha. You can't figure out a bloody thing from the voice. When will that twat of a director order the lights to be switched on? We can't see anything. Or maybe it's nothing to do with the director at all. Maybe the country is trying to conserve electricity – it's a periodic power outage, and they're burning candles in two hospitals, scores of kindergartens, three factories and a strategic missile unit . . .

By lunchtime my head hurt. I was still sitting in front of the monitor, and for a moment I fancied I saw Sashka Korostishevski coming up behind me. He was standing behind me and slyly, silently grinning. I whipped around. Malkin was standing there selecting the right smile.

'Hi, Alex!' A series of deformed smiles flashed under-neath his nose. He settled for the Broad Smile. The Broad Smile of the Friendly Boss.

'Hi, Steve,' I answered with a Ready Smile.

'You sure are working a lot.' He thrust out his lower lip and nodded his head.

I wasn't certain what he meant. That I'd been staring at the same screen all day long? Or that I was looking crap? I didn't know. I decided not to say anything.

'It's nearly lunchtime. Why don't we get a bite to eat?'

Right. Now he had me. This was a first.

'Sure, Steve,' I agreed.

He who takes a girl to dine also takes her to dance. Yesterday Kurochkin took me to dine, today Malkin. At this rate they'd soon be passing me from hand to hand.

But Malkin wasn't interested only in me. He was also interested in Kurochkin. That recent phone call was preying on his mind.

'Alex, have you know Mr Kurochkin for long?' We'd just sat at a table in the small room behind his office.

'We were on the same course at university.'

'No kidding!' Malkin brightened. 'I bet you've heard me say before that I went to school with Bill Hume.'

Cautiously I said, 'Yes, I've heard something about that.'

'What a great guy – a real American. I'll tell you about him some time. I'll be sure and do that. Anyway, I guess that means you and Mr Kurochkin are . . .' Malkin surprised me once again. I didn't think he was capable of abandoning his Hume as easily as that. 'I guess that means he knows you're working for our company?'

'Of course he does,' I said.

'Well?' Malkin took my elbow as if in confidence. 'Do you ever talk to him about it?'

I shrugged. 'Kurochkin has his own sources. Why would he start talking to me?'

'Oh no, that's not what I meant.' Malkin lifted his hands. 'Not at all. Although . . . well, that, too. And you're an interesting person to talk to, Alex. I've noticed that before, oh yes.' He waved his hand in front of my face and started laughing.

I don't like it when people talk with their hands, and I really can't stand it when they take me by the arm, pull at my jacket or try to give me a slap on the back. It's one thing if they just don't know what to do with their hands, but these days everyone's got a superficial grasp of NLP – neuro-linguistic programming. People don't convince you these days, they P-R-O-G-R-A-M-M-E you. They drop anchor. It's become easy to deal with them. Their behaviour is predictable and their reactions stereotypical. It's all incredibly boring and unpleasant.

'Kurochkin often meets with your compatriots.'

'Oh yes, he's got a really good reputation. In Washington they consider him a big friend of America . . .' Now Malkin obviously thought he'd blabbed more than he should. He laughed loudly and gave me an entirely inappropriate thump on the shoulder. And how would he know what they thought of Kurochkin in Wash - ington anyway? He was just puffing himself up.

'Really?' I enquired with polite surprise.

'Yes. But let's talk business, Alex. There's something else I wanted to talk to you about. Whatever your relationship with your friend, you might find a conversation about your career even more interesting, right? After all, you've been working for us for almost five years now.'

'Has it really been that long?' I asked in surprise.

'It sure has. You do a good job – I've always had my eye on you – but I can't shake the feeling we're not making full use of your potential. You've got more to give the company. Isn't that right?'

I noticed long ago that Malkin loved to ask slippery little questions you couldn't give a good answer to. If I had more to give, then why wasn't I giving it? If I didn't, then what good was I? NLP is odious – I was supposed to feel guilty before him and the company. In a case like this there's no need to reply. You're better off blurting out something meaningless and inoffensive. Let him think I was an idiot if that's what he wanted.

'I really rate the company's interests, Steve. That's something that really matters to me.'

I thrust out my lower lip and nodded like Malkin himself. Among our own people I couldn't have got away with it – they would see right through me. The Americans had fattened us on a diet of political correctness that our innermost beings rejected. But they themselves wolfed it down, no problem – the words crackled and crunched pleasantly behind their ears.

'You'll have an opportunity to give it some more thought. We're about to carry out a little *perestroika* of our own. You'll see some new departments appearing. We'd like you to take charge of one of them – the Department of Microstrategic Planning.'

'How interesting. What are we going to do?'

'Well, yes, of course, that's what I'm about to tell you,' said Steve.

And he told me how you can see a lot from Memphis, Tennessee, but not everything. Which is why the leadership, first and foremost the wise Bill Hume (a real American – I'll tell you about him some time), had decided to delegate some functions to subsidiary companies. Malkin spent a good ten minutes describing the structural changes that needed to be carried out and then repeated that they were offering me a department. I could see he didn't know much yet himself.

Suddenly I had a mad idea. 'That's great, Steve,' I said. 'Of course, I'll accept. It's a great honour for me.' It was the right thing to say. Poor Malkin didn't know what was coming. He stuck out his lower lip contentedly and gave me a thumbs up. 'But before I take on such a responsible position I'd like to take some leave.'

'Leave?'

'Yes, Steve. Two weeks, beginning tomorrow. I really need some time off right now.'

In the end, Malkin gave me the two weeks, although he had to think about it long and hard. He was probably pondering the enigmatic and incomprehensible Slav soul. When you offer someone a promotion, he should root around with his nose to the ground, straining his blood vessels, groaning and sweating and showing his bosses that they'd been right to choose him and not someone else. But what did he have here? A request for leave? A mad people.

* * *

It was a long time since Sinevusov and I had enjoyed a tête-à-tête at the same table. That this wasn't the table covered with papers and bureaucratic penholders in his one-time office on Volodymyr Street but an ordinary and hastily cleared little table in a watering hole in the Podolsk neighbourhood, set with two beers and pistachios in a chipped dull-blue saucer, but nothing seemed to have changed. Nor had the two problems before us that we were going to have to solve together. He was Sinevusov, I was Davidov, and once again we were divided by a table and the questions left unanswered twenty years before.

In Rabelais Sinevusov hadn't spoken. He had listened to Kurochkin, kept his silence and eaten.

'Why did you have to drag him into this?' I asked Yurka once we'd returned to the car. 'If you've contacted him, you may as well contact the others. The general, your Ryskalov, and the rest.'

'You're right,' Kurochkin agreed unexpectedly. 'But where can I find them?'

'Wherever you found Sinevusov.'

Kurochkin shook his head.

'Ryskalov was killed in a car crash in 1993; that's a fact. Their chief retired in the late 1980s and kicked the bucket soon after. Of the remaining three agents, two were transferred before the collapse, one to Murmansk, the other to Kyrgyzstan. They're both pensioners now. I checked. The fifth got the sack. He tried running a gang and for a while he handled two markets in the city and controlled a chain of filling stations, but it didn't last long. He was screwed by his own men. A tough business.'

'No joke,' I said. 'You were quick pulling your information together.'

'With these guys it's easy. They come from the system. It's harder with other people.'

'What about Sinevusov?'

'What do you mean? You've just seen him.'

'What's he doing?'

'I don't know.' Kurochkin shrugged. 'Why don't you ask him.'

'You mean you don't know?' I didn't believe him.

'He's not doing anything in particular. He's a pensioner, too, you know. What else do you want? Twenty years have gone by.'

'But he left the KGB a long time ago. It's been at least ten years, hasn't it?'

'Yes. It seems something happened. But how did you know?'

'It doesn't matter,' I said, paying Kurochkin back for his 'I don't know'. Kurochkin waggled his brows and feigned nonchalance, but he was obviously displeased. Nor did he like the fact that I knew something about Sinevusov and wouldn't tell him how. But what could I actually tell him? That one day I'd decided to have myself a bun and a cup of tea? It was ridiculous.

After I'd finalized matters with Malkin the day following our meeting and won my two weeks of freedom, I agreed to meet up with Sinevusov. Two weeks is a long time. Long enough to meet Mishka Reingarten and Kanyuka, find out whatever we didn't know about

Korostishevski and convince myself one more time that none of us had anything to do with the ultimatum or the disappearance of the money.

'Very Dostoevskian,' I said with a nod at the room. The room wasn't remotely Dostoevskian. It was just your average watering hole, moderately filthy and immoderately full of smoke, refuge of the local drunks and of the traders from Zhitni Market.

Sinevusov looked around the room, a group of young people – clearly students – briefly holding his eye, then shrugged. 'I don't like Dostoevsky.'

I didn't say anything, gave him time to graze on the nuts, one after the other, and drink some beer.

Finally, he continued. 'Dostoevsky was a wimp – a wimp and a coward. A brilliant coward. He broached such themes . . . plumbed such depths . . . it took your breath away. And then what? Nothing. He carefully tiptoed around it. Along the very edge, softly softly, so that, God save him, he wouldn't plant a foot wrong.'

'Such as?'

'What about Smerdyakov? Tell me, where's it, say, that Smerdyakovs get hanged? Karamazovs get hanged, but Smerdyakovs live happily ever after. Because the rules of our world are written and approved by Smerdyakovs. It's suffocating here for Karamazovs, but Smerdyakovs find it comfortable. Do you remember what he did to Ivan and how he framed Dmitri? Just masterful. Do you think a man like that would stick his head through a noose over such a trifle?'

'It wasn't exactly a trifle.'

91

'Not to anyone else, but to him it was a trifle. To him everything was permissible. That's the point.' Sinevusov looked me straight in the eye and asked sternly, 'Can't you see?'

'Who gave him permission?' I shuddered under his gaze.

'No, you can't see . . .' His gaze softened, the lines on his face smoothed out and formed a smile. A calm, clear smile. 'He allowed himself everything. He was his own supreme authority. There was no other. Now do you see? And Dostoevsky went and hanged him. And for what?' Suddenly Sinevusov broke into ear-splitting laughter. 'Because some Ivan Karamazov denied his words? What are words? They're like the wind; they blow and they disappear. And, for this, Smerdyakov hanged himself. He gave his life. He wouldn't have given a torn rouble that easily, but here . . . What sort of psychologist does that make of your Dostoevsky, eh?' Sinevusov didn't finish. He waved his arm contemptuously and reached for his beer. 'He was a wimp . . .'

He spoke firmly and confidently, and I could see he had carefully thought through everything he'd said. There was truth in his words, but it was the truth of our times, times that believed in nobody and nothing. Although who could say Dostoevsky's times were any different?

'Look,' whispered Sinevusov, leaving aside his beer and looking across the room at the large group of students was sitting at two tables that had been pushed together. They were drinking beer and having a quiet discussion. As often happens, the general conversation fragmented after a while, and the group split into smaller groups according to interests. It wouldn't have been worth the attention but for a short, energetic bloke with the look of an ageing Mephistopheles who was flitting among them. Half a glance was enough to see that he was a foreigner. Mephistopheles half sat with one group of students then another, constantly striking up conversations, asking questions and immediately jotting notes into a notebook.

'You see?' said Sinevusov, still whispering. 'There are hundreds of them here. I used to work at the Soros Foundation. I've seen my share.'

'Huh?' I said, mystified. 'What are you talking about?'

'He's a spy. It's a long time since I've come across such a colourful example. Watch – he could have stepped right out of a poster.'

Sitting across from me only moments before had been a home-grown Nietzschean, reader and commentator on the Russian classics, pensioner and nonentity; but just as soon as quarry flickered across his field of vision, his hunter's instinct had surfaced. Tiny caplets of venom appeared on Sinevusov's cheeks.

Unaware that a beast of prey was lurking near by, Mephistopheles was chatting away light heartedly with the students. He looked absurd and out-of-place.

'What does he want with the students?'

Sinevusov tore his gaze away from Mephistopheles and looked at me. All I had asked was one completely neutral question. But a sequence of other questions, although unspoken, was effortlessly discernible. Suddenly I saw an old paranoiac, unhinged by the world of spies, ready to dig away at any foreigner until under the dusky artificial tan he found the rapacious grin of a worldwide cabal. And he knew as much.

'Students?' repeated Sinevusov.

'Yes, what can they tell him?'

'They're not students. They're journalists. I know at least three of them. Not stars but not exactly bottom of the heap either. I can't imagine what the hell they're doing in this dump.'

'They're spying on the old goat.'

'And I'm trying to figure out who the old goat is,' snorted Sinevusov. He scowled. 'Davidov, I may strike you as an incurable maniac, but I've learned a thing or two, that's one; and two, it's a long time since I've been in the service, so espionage is no longer my concern. But if I see what I'm seeing then what am I to do? Deny what's before my very eyes? Kiev has become a hotbed of espionage. Everyone is here working against Russia: the French, the British, the Germans, the Poles. Not to mention the CIA. The Chinese are the only ones who are stealing local technology on the sly and don't care a toss about anything else. For now.'

'This one doesn't exactly look Chinese.'

'Well, the small fry are international. They gather rumours, gossip, search for compromising evidence. Anything that anyone else might want. Just like you and me, incidentally,' he said, taking an unexpected dig. 'Get a pen and write this down.'

From his jacket pocket Sinevusov took out a note-book and read, 'Reingarten, Mikhail Aleksandrovich. Born 1966. Diagnostic-Treatment and Scientific-Pedagogical Psychiatric Centre . . .'

'What?' I was confused.

'Frunze Street, 103.'

'Whatever . . . Scientific-Pedagogical . . .'

'Department four. Will you go?'

'I'll go tomorrow.'

'They don't have visiting hours tomorrow.'

'When do they have visiting hours?'

'Today.'

'You're saying I should go right now? Are you going, too?'

Sinevusov screwed up his left eye, tutted and shook his head.

'He's your friend, not mine. You haven't seen each other for ages, so go and visit him. You think I've any reason to go to the hospital, that I've forgotten something there?'

'I'll remind you what you've forgotten.' I nodded and got up from the table. 'Clearly your memory is failing you. You drove someone into a nuthouse for fifteen years – as good as killing him. And no one wants to remember. Pensioners . . .'

Outside it was beginning to get dark. Ice was floating in the dark mud in the flooded hollows of the pavement. Along the Upper Bank a solid line of cars was crawling slowly and gloomily by. I glanced through the window of the café. Sinevusov was standing with his arm across Mephistopheles' shoulder, saying something into his ear.

* * *

The day had disappeared. I walked around evening Podol, lazily ruminating about Mishka, Sinevusov, why the agent had wanted to meet in that particular filthy dive. A minute's telephone conversation would have sufficed to give me the number of the department where Mishka was being held. But Sinevusov made me waste an entire day. Or maybe he just wanted to talk. The whim of an old soldier, languishing from the boredom of forced idleness.

I told Sinevusov I would go see Reingarten, but visiting hours at the hospital were surely over by now, and it would be pointless going to Frunze Street. Instead, I turned on to the first side street, banished Sinevusov from my mind and breathed deeply the raw Podol air.

It had been a long time since I'd last been here. And it just happened to be during the lilac Podol sunsets I'd once loved more than anything. They come towards late February/early March when the snow is pressed up to the kerbs and hardened into black snowdrifts, and the smell of the day's thawed earth, smoke and old rotting fences rises above the asphalt. It's a time of cosmic solitude and metaphysical breakthroughs.

I slowly made my way along the Upper Bank to Frolov Street, occasionally casting a backwards glance at the black silhouette of Castle Hill perched carefully on the brink of the dense-mauve Kiev sky as it filled swiftly with darkness. In the intervening years nothing had changed here. Everything was the same, the street, Castle Hill, the heaviness of the raw evening sky. A savage canine howl could be heard from the direction of Schekavitsa Hill, and very close by, along Konstantine Street, the sound of automobiles at long last breaking free of the gridlock. When I reached Contract Square I stopped. The Dutch embassy was here. And the Church of the Assumption. 'The Lay of Prince Igor' came to mind: 'Igor rides along the Borichev to the Church of the Mother of God of Pirogoscha. The lands are victorious, the cities rejoice.' The lands are victorious . . . Show me these lands. Here was Borichev, the Church of the Mother of God that they'd finished rebuilding ten years earlier. It was a dead place. Here it seemed that everything was the same as it had ever been: the howling dogs, the old snow at the beginning of spring, the incredible colours of the evening sky. Even the smells were the same. Even Castle Hill. But the bridge to the cosmos had been destroyed. It was gone. There was no cosmos. No metaphysics.

I moved on. People were filing out of the church. At the entrance they turned back and crossed themselves, then went on their way quickly and silently. Here a woman came out, then another two women, then another. The next person to emerge was Associate Professor Nedremailo. I recognized him instantly, as if I'd been preparing for this meeting for the last twenty years. But he hadn't been, so without even noticing me he quickly stepped past, shielding his face with the collar of his coat.

He walked quickly, limping slightly and shivering as if it wasn't the usual zero degrees outside but a full-blown minus twenty-five. Evidently the professor had got thoroughly chilled inside the damp church. After the metro had been built in Podol the cellars of the surrounding houses began to flood in the spring. Greetings from the rivers Kiyanka and Glybochytsa, buried underground and in history.

Nedremailo headed for the metro. I followed him.

Even in 1984 we had no doubt that the whole thing – the searches, the arrests and what followed – had been cooked up by Nedremailo. First of all, the entire department knew the professor was an informer. How we knew this I've never found out, but everyone did. Second, it was Nedremailo who took the folder of papers from Sashka Korostishevski at an electrodes seminar. Korostishevski was keeping drafts in the folder: the draft ultimatum, estimates of the strength of the armed forces, sketches of campaign maps and lots of other working papers necessary for the admini-stration of a great power such as the Holy Roman Empire. Having quickly solved an electrodynamics problem Emperor Karl XX was preparing for battle. At the time we were doing all we could to ready ourselves for war: calling men to arms, conducting manoeuvres, riveting together tanks and howitzers in our factories. But not in Nedremailo's seminar. Who wanted to tangle with Nedremailo? Not Korostishevski. But it came to that. His folder was taken away, words were exchanged and the Holy Roman Empire was deprived of important documents. Who could have known this wasn't merely the beginning of our story but a preface? A prologue.

Then the bell rang and the seminar was over. Nedremailo left the classroom and headed down the corridor towards the stairwell, Korostishevski's folder tucked under his arm. We followed. We watched him carrying the folder; in his other hand the professor gripped a heavy briefcase. And as we watched we panicked and talked rubbish, constructing impossible plans, calculating how we could get the folder back. But Nedremailo quickly drew away from us, limping and slightly stooped.

He was walking just as quickly now. Past the tram stop, the grandmothers hawking sunflower seeds, the underground passage leading to the metro. Nedremailo mounted the steps to the Home Cooking Café. I entered the café right behind him.

What do associate professors eat for dinner? Borscht, dumplings with potato and mushrooms, sour-cucumber-and-sauerkraut salad. Bread. Beer. I confined myself to beer.

'Is this place free?'

Nedremailo raised his tired eyes to me. Then he looked pointedly around the half-empty dining-room. I acted like I didn't understand. I said, 'Thank you', and sat down across from him. Just over an hour ago Sinevusov and I had been sitting in exactly the same way. Ned-remailo shrugged and began eating his borscht.

When the professor turned to his dumplings I asked, 'Do you still lecture on electrodynamics in the radiophysics department?'

'When did you graduate?' He studied me but couldn't remember who I was.

'I didn't graduate. We were expelled in 1984 for truancy. Perhaps you recall . . .'

'No,' Nedremailo said and jerked his shoulder in irritation.

'. . . Korostishevski, Reingarten, Kurochkin . . .'

He certainly remembered Kurochkin.

'Ah yes, now I remember. That was an unpleasant business.' He rotated his fork, dumpling impaled at one end. 'But why truancy? As I recall, you were expelled on completely different grounds.'

'If you remember that much I'd like to ask you a favour. Could you give me the folder you took away from Korostishevski?'

'It's been many, many years since I've had that folder.' Nedremailo waved the fork and dumpling.

'Eat the dumpling,' I said. 'It will get cold. Or fly off your fork. And I'd hate it to end up in my beer. So where's the folder?'

'They took it away at the very first interrogation.'

'Interrogation? I always thought your dealings with the authorities went by another name.'

'Look here, what's your . . . ?'

'Davidov.'

'Right, Davidov. Look here, I'm not about to justify myself to you. You are not my judge. Is that clear?'

'It certainly is.'

'Then stop interrupting,' Nedremailo said quietly. 'I don't have to talk to you at all. Besides, it all happened a long time ago. Although I can understand why you're interested . . .'

'I certainly am,' I couldn't help saying.

'And I want you to know that I had nothing to do with that business. And I have nothing to do with it now.'

'Well, that just figures.' I crossed my arms and laughed. 'It just figures.'

'A lot of people in the department thought otherwise. A few people had words with me. They criticized me, and I couldn't even deny it. I was in a ridiculous position, you'll agree. But my hands were tied. I'd sworn an oath.'

'I see.'

'In short, yes, the KGB did come after you but not through me. You may think it ironic, but I really was summoned for interrogation a few days after your arrest, and that's when they took the folder. It was an unpleasant discussion.'

'Let's say that's what happened. But who was behind it then?' I sensed suddenly that he wasn't lying. 'No one gained from it. There was absolutely nothing to be gained.'

'I don't know. I do not know.'

'But you knew what was in the folder. You did open it, didn't you?'

'Yes, I opened it – although I actually forgot about it at first. I dumped it on the window ledge at home and forgot about it. Then a few days later your Kurochkin came along and asked me to give it back.'

'Yurka went to see you?' I was surprised. 'He didn't say. He's never even mentioned it.'

'Of course, I can't remember our exact conversation, but he came for the folder, that's for certain. I didn't give it to him. I said Korostishevski should get it himself. And afterwards, as you might expect, I had a look inside the folder.'

'And what did you think?'

'I didn't think anything. What was there to think about? I mean you were adults, second-year students, but you had butterflies fluttering around in your heads. You were just like nursery-school kids, I swear.'

'So you still had it.'

'Yes, I still had it. Korostishevski never turned up, and I had worries enough of my own. Really, was I to think of this folder to the exclusion of all else? Right. But they reminded me later on. "Where did you look? It was right under your nose. For ten days it was in your hands, and you couldn't even take a look . . ."'

'So you don't know who turned us in?'

Nedremailo shrugged.

'Can't you even guess?'

'Guesses aren't worth much in this business. No, I don't know.'

'All right then.' I got up. 'Hello to the radiophysics students.'

'I haven't taught there for nearly fifteen years.'

'Then what are you doing? You've got a long wait for your pension.'

'I do church work.' He jerked his shoulders again. 'That's just how it is.'

'I see. Well, enjoy your meal . . .'

'Davidov, wait. Like a bad student you lack patience. God only knows what you're trying to make yourself out to be. A private investigator or something.'

'I'm not a private investigator. I'm a private individual.'

It was a bad pun, but Nedremailo scarcely noticed.

'If I were you,' he was saying, 'I'd make a list of everyone who showed any interest in the matter. The broadest possible list. Maybe nine out of ten people on your list will only be there by chance. What matters is that the tenth doesn't go unnoticed. That's what I'd do. Then gradually narrow it down.'

'What exactly . . . ?' But then I understood. 'You mean it's not only Kurochkin and the KGB?'

'No, they're not the only ones.'

'So who else wanted the folder?'

'There was a girl in your group, if you remember . . .'

I knew whom he was talking about even before he gave her name.

'Natasha.'

'Yes, Belokrinitskaya.'

'Something's wrong here. Kurochkin and Belo - krinitskaya had nothing to do with the KGB or our arrest. Kurochkin was arrested himself, and Natasha . . . When did she come for the folder?'

Nedremailo sat quietly, arms folded across his chest, biting his lip intently and staring at the ceiling.

'Listen,' I said, surprised. 'Why did you tell me about Belokrinitskaya?'

He wasn't happy with the conversation. It would have been unpleasant for anyone in his situation. He could have cut it short, but he didn't.

'Because we both want the same thing. You want to find out what happened back then, right?'

'Yes.'

'So do I.'

'But what's it to you?'

'As a result of that business I had to leave the department.'

'Excuse me, but I find that rather hard to believe. You worked there for another six years.'

'I did. And it became harder with every year.'

I feigned sympathy. 'I see. The orgy of glasnost, the bacchanalia of democracy.'

'You don't see anything.' Wearily he waved his arm. 'When they take you by the throat and make you choose between your health, inasmuch as you've got any, or the life of your daughter and some treaty or other . . . you'll agree to whatever they want. Not that . . . And then, later, I didn't take any initiative. They asked; I answered. They said "Do this"; I did it. But as for me going to them and making a statement against someone else, that didn't happen. You can be sure of it.'

Nedremailo's mobile began ringing.

'Yes, yes,' he said, 'I'm free now. Come on over . . . to the metro.' He put his phone away. 'That was my daughter calling. Let's go.'

We went out on to the street. He gave me his business card.

'One more thing, Davidov. You can think whatever you want about me, but I want everything to be completely transparent. I need it as much as you do. Trust me. If there's anything you need, give me a call.'

Nedremailo made for the metro. Near the tram stop a woman in a dark coat and shawl went up to him, and together they descended into the underground passage.

* * *

'Did you see Reingarten yesterday?'

Kurochkin's call got me out of bed. Dawn was just beginning to break.

'Do all deputy premiers telephone at this hour, or is it my privilege to be dealing with an exceptional state servant? What time is it?'

'Did you go to the hospital or not?'

Finally I was awake, and awake I caught the note of barely checked irritation in Kurochkin's voice.

'No.'

'Why not? You told Sinevusov you were going to see Mishka.'

'I might have done. Or maybe that's just what he wanted to hear. Kurochkin, I've told you once and I'll tell you again, stop telling me what to do. I don't work for you. I'll do what I want to do. And I'm on leave.'

'Don't get carried away, Davidov,' advised Kurochkin after a weighty silence. 'I'm counting on you anyway.'

'Yurka, I promised to try to find out what's going on, not to run around buying cigarettes for Sinevusov. Let's talk tonight. Better still, tomorrow. I might have something to tell you by then.'

'OK then. Check your email.' Kurochkin sighed and hung up.

He had woken me up and for no good reason. I had hoped the conversation with Nedremailo would settle overnight and I might grasp the implications that had evaded me the evening before during our conversation at the Home Cooking Café. I was certain they were there. It often happens this way: I push a conversation into a distant box of my consciousness and forget about it until morning, then in the morning I take it out, cleaned and pressed, laced up and numbered. I have no idea what happens in there. I can't do it consciously. However much I try it doesn't work. But there had been something in the conversation with Nedremailo, a riddle that flickered past like a fleet shadow and disappeared. I'd been hoping to find it in the morning in an open box. But Kurochkin spoiled it. Damn him!

There had been curious flickers at several points in the professor's story. I was surprised to learn that Kurochkin had gone to him for Korostishevski's folder. Kurochkin knew Sashka wouldn't ask Nedremailo to return it. We all knew it, but Kurochkin was the only one who acted, even though they weren't close friends.

In fact, they weren't friends at all, but still Kuroch-kin tried to help him. Then there was the thing about Nedremailo's daughter. People in the department had called him a ladies' man to his face – he had three daughters. His eldest was seriously ill. She must be the one he referred to the night before. I don't know what made me latch on to this. And then there was Belo-krinitskaya. Nedremailo didn't actually say when she'd asked for the folder, but I wanted to know. I wasn't indifferent to anything about her. Not that I was a one-woman man. After all, it hadn't been love but a youthful infatuation tinted with rivalry and passion. I think she knew as much. Natasha was a smart girl. And I remem-bered her rather than the women that followed probably because Natasha was the emblem of those two short years at university. I probably wasn't the only one who felt that way. We were expelled during our second year, and a few weeks later we were living completely different lives.

I don't know how else to explain it. Once in the mid-1990s at a bar in a Moscow hotel I met an old black-marketeer (if anyone still remembers what that means). His name was Hussein. In the 1970s he started manufacturing and selling plastic lighters. The bodies were churned out in Baku and the metal components in Riga. The lighters were sold throughout the Soviet Union, in big cities and at train stations, and they sold particularly well in resorts. At the time Hussein had been living in Azerbaijan, where he was arrested and given fourteen years, but he was released after the start of perestroika. Then he moved to Uzbekistan and went into business again, but this time it wasn't going so well. Hussein had come to Moscow for money; he wanted to get a loan secured on his home and business. All evening he told me how he had done business in his day. He showed me a photocopy of a newspaper article a quarter of a century old. The article was about him. It said 'the illegal manufacture of material goods' by Hussein had cost the government several million roubles (the figure in the article was precise right down to the kopeck). Hussein was proud of the article, the figure and even his prison sentence. He was a spry, cheerful old man on the whole, and the only time he turned gloomy that evening was when the conversation turned to Kiev.

'I don't like Kiev,' he said resolutely and poured some vodka. 'I've only been there once. My wife and I spent two weeks in a hotel with a balcony that looked right out over the Dnieper. The hotel was a semi-circle right on the banks of the river –'

'Probably the Slavutych,' I mused.

'I can't remember. Maybe. It was September, warm and lovely. I would go out on to the balcony, and there before me was this beautiful, verdant city with all these churches. We ate only in restaurants and had ourselves a very relaxing time. That's how we spent those two weeks.'

'And then what?'

'Then I went home. And the next day I was arrested. So for the next fourteen years in prison I remembered that balcony and the river and the churches on the opposite bank . . . Forgive me, but I don't like Kiev.'

I felt like that about Belokrinitskaya, but in reverse. She'd left a long time ago. First she'd gone to Norway, but I no longer knew where she was or what she was doing.

Seven cups of coffee later – I didn't wash the cups; I lined them up on the kitchen table: four coffee cups left over from my parents' service, two tea cups purchased at random and one big mug – I put the conversation with Nedremailo back where it had come from: back into its box. And turned on the computer.

Another email addressed to Istemi had arrived, cc'd to: the President of the United Islamic Caliphates, Caliph Al-Ali; the Lama of Mongolia, Undur Gegen; and the Emperor of the Holy Roman Empire, Karl XX.

'My dear esteemed comrade monarchs, dictators and presidents,' wrote President of the Slovenorussian Federation, Stefan Betancourt, in a cavalier voice,

As you know, history with a capital H has come to an end. It has been deposited in a pawnshop for safe - keeping and scattered with mothballs. But our own history came to an end even before that, twenty years ago, so let's not flog a dead horse. Let it rest in peace. There is no one for us to bear grudges against and no one to petition for compensation for moral damages. And no reason for doing so. I, at any rate, have no intention of doing so. If anyone has any questions, I suggest that we meet. As for everyone else, please leave me in peace. According to the rules it is now my turn. I shall not take it, nor shall I pass it to the next player. I will tell you one more time: the game is over. Forget about it.

I read the letter once, then I read it again. It was written in a panic. If Kurochkin had written it by hand the letters would have jumped on the page, colliding with one another and sticking together in illegible lumps. He was thoroughly spooked. In a normal state of mind he simply couldn't have written so much nonsense in such a short space. And then there was this morning's telephone call. Something had happened. There was no doubt about it. Something seriously unpleasant. Far more serious than anything he had told me. If so, I ought to put some distance between us. Get away and watch what happened next from the sidelines. You can see better as an onlooker.

Not exactly a heroic attitude, I have to admit. Twenty years ago I would have behaved differently. I would have rushed to poor Kurochkin to find out what was wrong. I would have sifted through possible solutions, sought the right people, money, ways out. You don't abandon a friend in need . . . But it was all different now. Before ending up in my safe bottling factory I'd struggled against the current for six years, trying to surface for air right in the middle of the rapids. I couldn't do it. I couldn't swim free, but at least I didn't drown. I had worked for four private firms, in three of which I had been a founder member. We were beaten in different ways, but the end result was always the same. And if the first three times I remained steadfast, investing my strength, money and life in my friends, regardless of whether they were genuine friends or just happened to be on the same side of the line separating us from the bandits, cops and outright bad guys who came to take our business away, then the fourth time I didn't bother. The first three times, coupled with my observations of those around me, had been enough. So when Steve Malkin's predecessor offered me money and a job in exchange for information about my client firms I accepted the offer. And for five years now I had lived a peaceful life.

What Kurochkin shared with the Americans – or more importantly, his colleagues here – and what rules they played by, I didn't know, and I didn't want to know. There was no need for him to shout that the game was over. I could hear him. If it's over, then it's over. What was he shouting for?

I managed to convince myself. It wasn't too hard. I already knew I wasn't going to jump into the fire, not for chestnuts or bananas or fried baboons. I wouldn't jump in there for Kurochkin or anyone else. My instinct for self-preservation had not let me down yet. But I was ashamed. Even if you put aside an old friendship, however ephemeral and weakly demonstrable, I still owed a lot to Kurochkin. He'd stepped in for me more than once. Sometimes it was small stuff, but other times it was serious. And he brought me to Steve Malkin's office before Malkin himself knew he was coming to

Ukraine. Even my peaceful, comfortable existence I owed in part to him.

I skimmed the letter once more. Kurochkin had left all the email addresses visible: mine, the Hotmail address the ultimatum was sent from three days before and another, apparently Kanyuka's. Only three. Reingarten at Frunze 103 was unlikely to have access to email. I emailed Kanyuka: 'Vadik, we must meet. Davidov.' I didn't know where he lived or what he had been doing for the past ten years, but we had to meet. Then I found Nedremailo's business card, drank my eighth cup of coffee and dialled his home telephone number.

* * *

At about the same time the next day I was driving through the dreary watercolour landscape of Kirovohrad Province. A dirty March sky swollen with heavy water blended into the muddy snow of the endless fields. Also travelling in my car were a one-legged Chechen, his wife and her sister. I was taking them to Crimea. The Chechen's name was Vakha. He rode the whole way in the back seat, silent and with eyes half closed. He was obviously from the ranks of people accustomed to giving orders not receiving them, but things had not gone his way, and for the time being he was prepared to play along. Patiently he endured everything that was happening to him and around him, including this trip. His wife Larissa didn't speak either. Her sister Vera was the only one who didn't wish to keep silent, and she chattered enough for the three of them. Either she was recalling how the entire family had once travelled to Crimea along this very road or she was telling her sister something about their mutual acquaintances . . . I'm not too keen on garrulous women, but if it hadn't been for Vera the journey would have been a lot harder.

Larissa and Vera were twins. I estimated that they were somewhere around twenty-six to twenty-eight years of age, but Larissa looked forty, and Vera – if you felt generous – could pass for twenty. They were very much alike. Like mother and daughter. They'd had an older sister, the one Nedremailo had touched on vaguely in our conversation. After an illness lasting a number of years she died when she was still a child. Her sisters could barely remember her.

This unexpected trip had come about as a direct result of my phone call to Nedremailo. I'd gone to see him in the evening, but we weren't able to talk. The professor and his family were trying to solve a problem that wasn't quite clear to me: how to get Larissa's husband to Crimea, to the village of Vostochni not far from the city of Stary Krym. I had the time, I was ready to get out of Kiev for a while and you could do worse than Crimea for a holiday. It might have been freezing outside, but at least it was March. I decided I'd rather travel in company than alone, so the next morning I collected Nedremailo's daughters and son-in-law and sped south.

I didn't realize Larissa's husband was a Chechen, and only when he came out of the building did I see what was troubling Nedremailo and his daughters.

Vakha bore an astonishing resemblance to the Chechen guerrilla Shamil Basayev, whose unforgettable image had dazzled Russian journalists with love and awe during the first half of the 1990s. He was short in stature, lean and fit, his face hidden by a thick, curling, well-groomed beard and his head carefully shaved. Across his shoulder he'd thrown an old much-laundered officer's pea coat. Vakha leaned on a crutch with one arm, his other resting on Larissa's shoulder. Later Vera told me their story and much more. But that morning, at the entrance to their nine-storey apartment building on South Borschagovka, the last thing on my mind as I helped shove suitcases and bags into the boot was that she and I might have a mutual 'later'.

We reached Vostochni without misadventure – no one stopped us and checked our documents. I would have cast those seven hours behind the wheel from my memory altogether had we not made a stop of no more than fifteen minutes just before Melitopol. We stopped to eat. Vakha refused to get out and ate in the car, and Larissa stayed with her husband. Vera and I took a table in a small roadside café. Only now was I getting a proper look at her. I'd never seen Vera before, but something endlessly familiar played around the features of her face and echoed faintly in her voice and her very manner of speaking.

'You must be tired of my chatter,' Vera said. 'I usually don't talk so much, but I'm making an effort today for Larissa. Perhaps it's not making any difference, but I thought the journey would be easier for her if I reminisced about our childhood. We really did travel a lot to Crimea. But it doesn't seem to have done any good. She came home a changed person.'

'Came home from where?' I asked politely. I wasn't that interested in Larissa's life story. I was interested in Vera.

'From Chechnya. You mean you didn't know?'

'Ah . . .' I started in embarrassment. 'No, I didn't. What was she doing there?'

'It's a long story. We don't have much time now, but I'll tell you later some time.'

She was right. We didn't have much time. Hurriedly we gulped down our chicken soup and tucked into the overdone chicken legs and rice – for some reason the café only served chicken.

Then it was time to go back to the car.

Suddenly it dawned on me. 'Vera,' I said. 'You look astonishingly like an old classmate of mine.'

'Who?'

'You wouldn't know her. Natasha Belokrinitskaya.'

'I know Nastashka very well. All our relatives used to tell our parents we looked like her. "Your girls were poured from the same mould as Natasha." She's seven years older so it was a natural comparison.'

'You know her?' I was amazed.

'Our mothers are first cousins, so we're second cousins.'

'Has she ever been to your home?'

'Not that often, but she's been there.' Vera got up. 'Shall we? It's time we were off.'

We went outside. The sea could already be felt close by. A gentle mild spring breeze ruffled the air. It smelled of the sea and melting snow and grasses. Where do grasses come from in March? I don't know. I was standing at the door to the café watching Vera get into the car. Something had changed, decisively and irretrievably. Within and without. Only the sky remained the same – heavy, wet, grey and endlessly familiar. I had spent years beneath this sky. No, more than that. I had spent a lifetime beneath it. Once upon a time, before I'd begun trading in American fizzy drinks, Istemi's horsemen had swept beneath this sky, horsemen who were as light as death and as fast as time.

* * *

We reached Vostochni at dusk. Vakha was expected. I don't know who they were, friends or relatives, but they met him noisily and joyfully. I was allowed to stay the night, which was all that I wanted. I was very tired. Larissa didn't talk that evening, the same as during the day, the same as always. Vera, finding herself surrounded by people she didn't know and not knowing their language, suddenly lost her bearings. In the morning I asked her what her plans were.

'I was going to stay on for a week and help Larissa settle in, but now I'm not sure what to do with myself. It's not at all what I'd expected.'

'Would you like to go to the sea?'

'I'd love to,' she said happily. 'When are you going?'

'Right now.'

No one tried to stop us. I had a good look at Vostochni as we drove away; it was a typical Tatar village. Many settlements like this had sprung up in Crimea in recent years. The sense of poverty and despair that stifled them in the early 1990s was gone. People obviously had some money now and confidence in themselves. Even the Chechens were catching up. How would it all end?

'What does Larissa think about this move?' I asked as the road followed a bend and Vostochni disappeared behind a rare line of trees.

'Nothing. I think it's all the same to her. I said I'd tell you how Larissa married Vakha. We need something to do on the road, and there isn't a radio.'

'Indeed,' I agreed.

Vera began telling me her sister's story when we were getting on to the motorway between Stary Krym and Theodosia, and by the time she finished we had passed Alushta. We didn't get out at Theodosia, but we did go for a walk along the bar-infested seaside at Koktebel, and we had lunch in Sudak. Then Vera called home and told her father she had left Vostochni but was going to spend a couple of days in Crimea, and I checked my email. I was waiting to hear from Kanyuka, but he was maintaining his silence. Instead of a letter from Kanyuka I found a demand from Kurochkin either to meet him immediately or to contact him straight away. I wasn't going to do either. What did I care about Kurochkin now that I was travelling through spring-time Crimea with Vera alongside me – and her resemblance to Natasha Belokrinitskaya had already become almost inconsequential. Vera had been telling me about Larissa for several hours, but, strangely, this grave account didn't spoil our journey to Yalta or the following days in Crimea. As they say, it happened a long time ago and to somebody else, so what can you do about it now? There was Kurochkin, tearing about the cold, sleety streets of Kiev hunting for me, while I was . . . Well, never mind, he could wait a few more days. I decided to give him a ring when I got back home. Even though my conscience was still bothering me about letting a friend down, the situation would be clearer then.

The way Vera talked wasn't exactly confusing, but neither was her account neat and tidy. As she related a particular episode she might leap forward a couple of years or go back in time just to pick up an important detail. At times I didn't confine myself to the role of listener, and then our conversation would stray far from Larissa's fate. I've already forgotten many details of her story, and some I don't want to remember.

'It began when Larissa was abducted. Ten years ago.'

'In Kiev?' I asked in surprise.

'No, Moscow. She was kidnapped from a competition.'

At which point I understood it hadn't begun ten years ago but much earlier.

Vera and Larissa had looked alike from earliest childhood. But they were alike only on the outside. Larissa seemed older. She was reserved and only reluctantly did she let her parents and relatives close, whereas the role of beloved child was performed consummately by Vera. When they were around five years of age the girls began to study music. With Vera it was immediately obvious that while she would have loved to have pleased her parents she was little inclined towards the fine arts, so much so that to expect anything from her in this area was simply inhumane. And they left her in peace. With Larissa it was more complicated. It was discovered that the little girl had perfect pitch. At a music-school audition the commission members played various musical phrases, some quite complicated, and the child was able to reproduce them quickly and without mistakes. Even then she had a powerful hand that seemed designed for playing the violin. She was assigned to a violin class. But the problem wasn't merely that Larissa couldn't bear the instrument, it was that she quietly but passionately detested this whole business of music, and she resisted it in every way she could.

The war between parents and child lasted nearly four years and ended in total victory for Larissa. Her parents surrendered. Over time Larissa had grown into a hardened warrior. She now had a plan of which her victory over music was the first point. To fulfil the second point she enrolled in judo classes. By the time she finished school Larissa had battled her way to black belt. Vera tagged along with her sister to the sports hall a few times, but the sight of Larissa in a *judogi* didn't inspire her. And the throws, grapples, strikes, defences, they didn't scare Vera off, but they didn't draw her in either. Hers was a clear, analytical intellect, and she had a tangibly abstract mind. When they finished school, Vera enrolled in the university physics department; Larissa in the Institute of Physical Education.

In early September 1993, before Vera had even learned to navigate the tangled corridors of the laboratory building at Kiev's physics department, her sister went to Moscow for an international judo competition. She didn't come back. The trainers and the girls on her team neither knew nor understood what had happened. Larissa had been with everyone else in the gymnasium, she was seen in the changing room, and someone even noticed her walking towards the exit of the sports complex. Alone. But Larissa wasn't seen back at the hotel. Naturally they informed the police of her disappearance. And the Moscow police – despite their reassurances along the lines of 'Don't worry, your girl will turn up. The little wrestler's probably gone on a spree with the men. Give her a week, and she'll be back without any help from us. What's the hurry?' – reluctantly took the statement. Apparently they even took it upon themselves to search for Larissa. But their searches didn't turn anything up.

In the end, the Russian guardians of law and order were at least partly right. Larissa did turn up by herself. Exactly three years later, in September 1996, she telephoned home. Nedremailo picked up the receiver.

'Papa, this is Larissa. I'm in Grozny. Don't worry, everything's OK.'

It's possible that Larissa said more, but the professor didn't last that long. He collapsed in a dead faint after her first few words.

All that time the family had been searching for Larissa. It hadn't taken long to find out that she was in Chechnya. There had been a phone call. A man had rung. He spoke Russian but with a very heavy Ukrainian accent. During the course of the conversation Nedremailo switched to Ukrainian, but the caller stated right away that he didn't understand that language. His speech was vague and muddled somehow. He didn't ask for money in so many words, but he implied that Nedremailo's daughter would require assistance to get away. He firmly advised against contacting the authorities, but Nedremailo ignored this advice. He was accustomed to relying on the state, so to the Russian special services he added the Ukrainian Security Service, the Church and the Ukrainian Ministry of Foreign Affairs. He gave no peace to the Russian and Ukrainian ambassadors, the Red Cross people or any international organization he could get hold of. But to no avail. Nedremailo was for ever travelling to Moscow, and twice he tried to go to Chechnya, but he wasn't allowed beyond Mosdok a few kilometres from the border. Nedremailo told everyone around him that he was hopeful, but he hesitated to ask himself just what he was hoping for.

After the first phone call from Larissa several others followed. The war was over, and she and her husband were getting ready to leave Chechnya. She needed assistance and not just money. Paying all the fees and preparing to move took around a year. Then Larissa and Vakha bought half a house outside Moscow and settled in Russia.

Nedremailo went to see his daughter several times and came back looking glum. His child's life in Russia was not working out. The authorities didn't want to register them as residents, there wasn't any work, the neighbours watched them like wolves and once a week – as regular as clockwork – the cops would come to check their documents. And if the cops urgently needed money they might even drop by after hours. Vakha had friends in the next village. When these friends were banged up they knew they had to move on. They sold their half of the house and moved to Odessa.

In Odessa they lasted longer, but they encountered the same problems – the police, neighbours, work. Vakha needed to recuperate. The health and nerves of the former Chechen fighter were absolutely shot. Once, when Vera and her father went to visit Larissa, she saw how the militant mujahid went about decapitating a chicken destined for the lunch broth. They were living in a typical city apartment, so Vakha decided it would be easier to deal with the bird in the bathroom. As there wasn't a suitable axe to be found the deed had to be done with a knife. But the Ukrainian cock was extremely tenacious, and Vakha the Mussulman made a terrible butcher. Not yet done for, the cock escaped from under the knife and flew with a screech into the room. Spraying blood all over the walls and ceiling, it fled on to the balcony where it leaped across to the neighbours, frightening their children and grandmother half to death. The bird carried on squawking until, in a swift and practised movement, the neighbour wrung its neck.

For a long time Vakha sat mutely on the sofa, his face so pale it was blue-grey. He rocked to and fro, at times lowering his head below his knees. Then he looked at Vera and shrugged. 'I told her I couldn't do it. I can't bear the sight of blood.' At that moment Vera caught sight of her sister's face. An expression of dark satisfaction flashed across it and immediately disappeared.

The affair with the cock ended in the usual way – the quarrel with the neighbours, the police, the document check. The policeman from the precinct shuffled slowly between bathroom and balcony, scrutinizing the bloodstains and waggling his brows in consternation. 'Whose throat have you slashed here? You'd do well to come clean voluntarily – we'll find out anyway.' Instead of the usual fifty grivnas they had to pay seventy, all that they had.

After Vera finished her dissertation she found a post-doctoral post in Germany and spent a year in Western Europe. Larissa and Vakha moved in with her father in Kiev. It got a little easier then, but it was still impossible to find a job for Vakha. What could they do? He couldn't spend the rest of his life sitting at home – he was a healthy man, even if he only had one leg. Then a friend of Vakha's turned up from somewhere. He was hauling nuts in GAZelle minibuses and selling them in

Kiev, Minsk and Latvia. It was a proper business, nothing criminal about it, and the people involved were all his own men – Chechens. And they all lived together. Just like they used to do.

'So now what?' I asked Vera, as if I hadn't bid farewell to Larissa and Vakha that very morning in front of their new home in Vostochni.

'Wait and see,' she said with a shrug. 'Maybe they'll put down roots, maybe they won't . . . Who knows. It's hard being away from home,' Vera concluded unexpectedly. Over the past two years she had acquired experience of her own. It wasn't the same kind of experience as Larissa and Vakha's, not at all. But that's how experience is; everyone has their own.

After a long pause I nodded at a road sign. 'We'll be in Yalta soon. Shall we spend the night there?'

'Let's. But can you choose the hotel? I never get it right. I remember this one hotel, it was called the Oreanda . . .'

Suddenly I had an idea. 'I know. Last autumn our chiefs held a managerial conference for the Eastern European branches at the Levantine.'

'Where's that?'

'On the waterfront just after the Oreanda. It's excellent. The money's Russian, the service Ukrainian.'

'I can see it now . . .'

'No need to be sarcastic. It's seriously business class. From autumn to spring it's just wonderful.'

'And in the summer?'

'I wouldn't stay there during the summer. The

windows look out over the sea, to the south-east, and I don't like it when the sun blazes through the windows, especially in the morning. There you are, sleeping, and suddenly it's like someone's turned a light on inside your head. Even if you hide the sun behind heavy drapes and the room has air conditioning, I still don't like it. In the south, windows should look on to tennis courts . . .'

'. . . with palms and fountains and peacocks.'

'Yes. With palms and fountains. And peacocks – except at night the peacocks should be blindfolded or wear little hoods over their heads so they won't noisily greet the dawn.'

We cruised through the city on the south coastal highway, and then, weaving through the colonnades of sanatoriums and guesthouses, we made our way down almost to the sea itself. Just before the waterfront we turned into the Levant. We had arrived.

It was growing dark in the east and the sky was turning a deep blue. Across the sea and shoreline lay the first shadows of March twilight. The sound of waves breaking gently on the shingle was just audible. We took two small rooms on the first floor, left our things and went into the town.

By the end of that first joyful year after I got out of the army I suddenly realized there were areas of Kiev I knew my way around perfectly at night but never went to during the day and would scarcely even recognize. Yalta was like that. For me it has always been a nocturnal city, its streets and buildings presenting themselves not as crumbling façades, a pastiche of architectural styles and the sight of underwear drying on balconies but as a symphony of lights – street lamps, windows, fiery lines of night-time advertisements, ships at anchor languishing in port and, finally, the moon. At night my judgement becomes clearer, and I find my way more surely, through everything – the flashing lights of cities, the cities themselves and the people who inhabit them. Night pares away the unnecessary and leaves behind what matters.

An hour and a half before dawn we returned to the hotel. Even though I'd spent two days behind the wheel and hadn't slept a wink all night, I was ready to jump right back up again and drive off somewhere, go swimming or walking, anywhere I felt like going. The sense of freedom I'd thought long forgotten was back. Routine no longer existed, no regular responsibilities or commitments enslaved my liberty. I felt a sense of power; I'd gained power over my circumstances. It was no longer I who depended on circumstances, but circumstances that depended on me. And this was all down to a petite woman with chestnut hair and dark-brown eyes that reflected the cool shadows of a springtime night in Crimea.

In the morning we drove to the peak of Ai Petri. In the Crimean Mountains it was still winter. The snow lay wetly on the mountain plateau and above heavy flocks of fog swept swiftly and silently. At the meteorological station children and adults were bustling around and dogs were barking. Slowly we passed by a small ugly bazaar, continued north a few more kilometres, and then I stopped the car.

A sharp, penetrating wind sliced my face. The mountain slopes bristled with the dark green of pine. On the slanting dome of one of the summits a few gloomy structures jutted out – scattered caravans and radar sets.

'People certainly know how to spoil . . . everything,' said Vera suddenly. 'They make it ugly with their very presence. The hills, the sea . . . how beautiful it was here without us. We're probably a disease, a virus. We've contaminated the Earth and won't rest until we've destroyed it all.'

I didn't tell her, but I recalled having similar ideas on Kamchatka some fifteen years before. I'd clambered up an unnamed volcano and looked out with a sense of anguish upon the unsullied Breughelian greenery of the coast near the smooth-sloped Avachinsky volcano and its neighbours and then upon the filthy city, a disgusting fungus that had sprouted along the coast with jerry-built five-storey buildings, their panels cracking and the black and greasy smoke from the boilers . . .

'But how beautiful the horsemen looked here.'

'The horsemen?' said Vera without comprehension.

'The horsemen of Istemi,' I said, opening the car door. 'Let's go. I'll tell you about it on the road. Today it's my turn to tell stories.'

We headed further north then around in a big loop and returned to Yalta after lunch. I told Vera the entire story, from the very beginning up to the events of three days ago and my conversation with her father at the Home Cooking Café in Podol. I didn't mention that until very recently I had considered the professor to be the instigator of all our troubles, nor did I mention his connection to the KGB. The first point was my error, and the second no longer mattered.

'Strange.' Vera shook her head. 'I knew bits of this. I must have been eight when my father came home and said some students had been expelled for "a game with political implications". I never understood what it meant, but I remembered the words exactly: a game with political implications. How stupid . . . Incidentally, I've read the ultimatum, but that was later, much later.'

'Korostishevski's ultimatum?'

'Alex, I didn't know everyone's last names. It was the ultimatum of some Emperor Karl –'

'Karl XX: Korostishevski. How did you end up seeing it?'

'Natasha showed me. Natasha Belokrinitskaya. You know her.'

'Yes, yes, I know. But how did she get hold of it?'

'Ask her. I've got her telephone number. My address book is in Kiev, but when we get back I'll give it to you. I have her address, too. She left Europe for the States five years ago now. She works at the Massachusetts Institute of Technology. And it's ages since she's been Belokrinitskaya.'

'I'll be sure to ask her,' I said, shaking my head just like Vera had. 'Strange.'

When we got back to Yalta I checked my email. This

time there was nothing from Kurochkin, but Kanyuka had responded. 'I'm in Zaporozhye,' he wrote. 'I'd love to talk to you, see you, etc., but not if you're on Kurochkin's business. He's been burying me with his dispatches, but I have no intention of reading them, and I don't want even want to hear about that animal.' Kanyuka left his mobile number, and I called him straight away. We agreed to meet the day after next at his place. It needed to be soon because he was going away on a business trip, and I didn't want to postpone the meeting for a long time.

Vera and I stayed on in Yalta for a day and a half in all. That evening we went back into town – but this time we returned before it got late.

In the morning a pale-grey veil was stretched across the east, and the small matte globe of the sun was scarcely discernible. I lay motionless, gazing at the morning sun; the broad window, broad as the wall, and its drawn curtains; the armchair with Vera's jeans, jumper and blouse; and the pillow with the small depression where she had slept. She had slept there, and the pillow faithfully preserved the imprint of her head. On my fingers I could still feel the tender warmth of her skin, and on my lips there was still the faintest taste of blackcurrant, the taste of her lips. The sound of water could just be heard beyond the door to the shower room. I lay there peacefully; peacefully ran the water; the peaceful sun was rising beyond the low clouds. I suppose it was happiness. I don't know. I didn't get the chance to digest it fully. There was a remote on the bedside table, and I idly switched on the television. I turned the sound off and surfed channels until I came to the Ukrainian news. I rarely watch the news – and not just the Ukrainian news but any news – so the jowly faces of our politicians speechifying within mottled gold interiors were for the most part unfamiliar to me. On the screen one head replaced another and the cheerless landscapes outside of Kiev flashed by along with signage showing the town names. Occasionally the anchorman would surface to say a few words. Near the end of the broadcast he lingered a little longer than usual, and I decided he was bidding the audience goodbye and asking them not to change the channel because the advertisement would be followed immediately by the weather forecast and an entertaining family talk show. But I was wrong. Instead of an advertisement I saw Kurochkin. It was an old clip from his days as Deputy Premier – they probably couldn't find anything more recent. Kurochkin was vigorously holding forth on the steps to the Cabinet of Ministers. Then the screen flashed to a bank sign – and I realized it was Kurochkin's bank – and someone was waving his arm in protest before the camera, making it clear there would be no comment. The footage immediately cut to the sign of the General Prosecutor's Office. I reached for the remote but accidentally dropped it, and when I finally picked it up and turned on the sound all I could see were the final shots of the report: yellow earth, white houses with flat roofs and the flag of Israel in the foreground.

When Vera emerged from the shower I was

attentively watching a commercial for German lemon-ade. She stopped and gave me a bemused look.

'Are your rivals on the offensive?'

'I've just seen Kurochkin on TV,' I said, turning off the television. I wished I'd never even turned it on – it had spoiled my mood for the rest of the day.

'Your Kurochkin?'

'Mine. If I've decoded this pantomime correctly, he's got into trouble and fled to Israel.'

'Did they say what kind of trouble?'

'They might have done, but I didn't hear. "There was an old monkey who had a clogged ear" – especially when he tried to watch TV without any sound.'

'Wait until the next news broadcast – if it's important.'

'It's important all right. But not important enough to spend the day glued to the box. I'll ask Kanyuka about it tomorrow. He'll probably know more than the journalists do.'

Having uttered these prophetic words, I spent almost two hours in front of the screen, flipping from one news broadcast to another. Different things were being said about Kurochkin: they muddled his position, age, even his name, calling him first Yuri then Igor. Varying accounts were given of his urgent departure for Israel – I hadn't been wrong about that. The one statement that remained consistent throughout the reports went something like, 'The prosecutor's office is conducting an inquiry into the legitimacy of agreements signed by Kurochkin during his tenure in the Cabinet of Ministers.' The feeling of guilt that had flowed over me (after all, he'd asked me to get in touch; maybe I could have helped him) receded somewhat when I heard this. I couldn't have helped him after all.

* * *

Kanyuka had grown fat. A bald little man with drooping cheeks, double chin and eyes where the life had been snuffed out for ever, he pressed me against his immense paunch at the door to a Zaporozhian diner. He uttered a few well-worn stock phrases, but he seemed genuinely touched, and his words were sincere. It was more than a decade since we'd last met when we'd been around twenty-five. If I hadn't known how old he was I'd have put him at fifty, he'd aged that much. In our country business is bad for your health.

'I don't think you've met. This is Vera, Nedremailo's daughter.'

'What a last name!' roared Kanyuka. 'Just the sound of it makes me break out in a cold sweat.'

'Don't overdo it now.' I thumped his back. 'This your place?'

'You guessed it. You were always good at that. Let's go in and you can have yourselves something to eat after your journey. It's not exactly Maxim's, but I can feed my own.'

Kanyuka had a small chain of cafés within Zaporozhye and the surrounding area. He would be an ideal client for my firm. I should have got him to sign a contract and serve our cola; we could beat any competitor's price. Taste and quality, no; price, yes. But I didn't say anything about cola. Instead I asked Vadik about Kurochkin.

'Our Kurochkin has really landed himself in it now. The worthless bastard has finally jumped in the shit. The silly grasshopper. Bloody hope of our young democracy,' Kanyuka said with satisfaction and poured the vodka.

'I'm driving, Vadik.' I had to push my glass aside.

'And the lady? Is she driving, too?'

'The lady can have a drink,' replied Vera. 'But just a little, thanks.'

'Here's to us then.' Kanyuka raised his glass. 'To us, knocked around by this bloody life in this bloody country . . . three times I've been ruined. I've lost everything, everything but my debts. My debts were rescued like children from a burning house – last time thanks to that Doberman Pinscher Kurochkin. But, what the hell, I'm living the way they taught us to do in the army. I've fallen down and pulled myself back up again. So what's the lady do?'

'She's a physicist,' I said and raised my glass of tomato juice. 'Vadik, that toast . . .'

'Huh? It was to us. What didn't you understand? To big businessmen who used to be physicists and to physicists with a future. With a big future, that is.'

'Just how did Kurochkin screw you over?' I asked when I'd finished eating the salad, pork chop and fried potatoes with mushrooms, and when the vodka, thanks to Kanyuka's efforts, was almost gone. 'What's going on with him?'

'It's simple. The mine he planted beneath his feet fifteen years ago, the one he's thrived on like a fungus on a rotted tree stump, it's finally exploded, and the shit is flying. And he's about to crash down on top of us and spin us a sob story. It should be fascinating. Kurochkin's always made such a big deal about being his own man. "I'm not right or left. I have no ties to corporate interests. I don't depend on anybody – I'm an honest man."'

'But the truth is ?'

'The truth is this honest man was reared by the KGB. First the KGB, then the Ukrainians. Then he got big enough to stand on his own two feet, but the ties are still there.'

'But they think he's pro-American in the States,' I said, remembering Malkin's fervent monologue of the previous week.

'Sure they do. But you don't remember Kurochkin. He's everyone's friend. He thinks everyone else is an idiot, and he's the smartest one of all. But they're not idiots. And I can't be the only one he's got his teeth into. But never again. They've got all they want now from Kurochkin – and not just the Cheka secret police. There are others, too, but the game's up, and he's really going to get it. There's no one backing him up any more but a handful of Chekists. And after fifteen-odd years they must be sick to death of him. Chances are that's what they'll do.'

'As far as the secret police are concerned, let's just say that's speculation on your part. So what was the problem? Can you tell me?'

'There shouldn't have been any problem at all, Davidov. There was a small factory outside Kiev that I wanted to buy from the state – or, rather, privatize. That's all. Kurochkin was Deputy Premier at the time. I don't know what the hell made me get in touch with him – I could have handled it by myself, but I thought I'd get myself some protection. He said, "Bring your money out into the open. We're creating a transparent economy. But I'll help you and press the right buttons." Like an idiot I did everything he said. After all, he was an old friend, and he was running the show around here. I was losing almost 10 per cent as it was, but right there and then everyone swooped down on me: the tax police, the Economic Crime Office, state security, funds, schmunds and a few moronic bandits . . . You know what he did? He used me to settle his debts.'

'No way. That doesn't hang together somehow . . .'

'As ever, Kurochkin is as white as snow. He said, "You attracted attention to yourself. You should have been more careful." And he washed his hands of me.'

'Maybe it didn't have anything to do with him?'

'In that case he could at least have given me a hand. But no . . . And later on, when the dust settled, I made enquiries. Everything pointed to him. I can tell you don't believe me.'

'Not exactly.'

'I can't prove anything – there's nothing in writing – but my advice is to steer clear of him. Don't even get close. Not just because he's got problems right now, they're nothing to do with you anyway. It's when he's strong and things are going his way that Kurochkin is dangerous. The bait is on the hook, the nets are in place. He's like a spider – he devours everything within reach.'

'What a picture.' I laughed. 'But what's the point of the ultimatum then? You got a copy, right?'

'Yes. I couldn't believe my eyes when I read it – straight from our snot-nosed childhood and all. But that's something else. Entirely.'

'That's what I'm saying. There are things you don't know –'

'Certainly,' interrupted Kanyuka. 'And lots of them. But I know what matters – that Kurochkin's a piece of shit, and the security services are shaking him down for good reason. The rest is just details. Now, come clean. Did you send it?'

'The ultimatum? You're kidding. Kurochkin asked me to find the author . . . that is, not the author – we all know who wrote it – he asked me to find out who sent it. You know, he thought it might be Korostishevski, and he wasn't fooling around.'

'Alex, I've got one more thing to say about Kuroch-kin, and then we won't talk about him anymore, OK? He's not worth it. But the fact that he's even afraid of Sashka Korostishevski – God rest his soul, may he rest in peace and all that, he was a lovely bloke – the fact that he's afraid of Sashka's ghost tells you a lot. Just think about it. He's charming, certainly, and he wears a velvet glove, yes, but heaven forbid you should –'

'Vadik, I've known him for more than twenty years and he's never –'

'That only means you don't know everything. Or your time hasn't come yet. But enough of that. Let's talk about something more pleasant. Tell me,' he said, turning to Vera, 'how's your father getting on? I think about him now and again.'

* * *

It was late at night when I dropped Vera off on South Borschagovka. We agreed to talk the next day and quickly said goodbye. I still had another week of leave, and she had ten days before she left for Germany.

The whole week we were away it had been raining in the city. The rains had finally melted away the snow. Although the weather forecasts still reported that tiresome old refrain 'Around zero in the capital, wind northerly changing to north-easterly, possible precipitation', it was clear that spring had arrived. Only the wind had yet to surrender.

The next day I left the house in the morning and spent the day wandering aimlessly. When I had felt like this in the past I would jump into the car late at night, get on to the ring road and let myself race along, cleaving through the changeable, swampy night. Then, dropping my speed a little, I would return to the city and zigzag at length inside the triangle between Lukyanovka, St Sofia and the Botanical Gardens. Occasionally I went to Podol, less often to Pechersk. At this hour the roads were peaceful, travelled only by taxi drivers and other drivers like myself, petrol heads crazed with loneliness and the senselessness of existence. While waiting for the light to change I would study their greyish faces, their brows drawn in torment. Some moved their lips, talking to themselves, filling the emptiness with the sound of their own voices – they had nothing else to fill it with. Frequently I saw women at the wheel. Office managers. Plasticine businesswomen absorbed in business – usually not their own but somebody else's – and absorbed far more deeply than it warranted. Some had spent the day in negotiations and meetings. The bird language of negotiations was long the only language they could use or understand without an interpreter. This nocturnal journey was a crack in the unified, unshakeable picture of their world. In the morning they would hurriedly paint it out, but in another week or two it would once again mar the façade of the tidy little house they had built exactly according the instructions in glossy magazines. Even at night they concentrated on the road as if it would lead them to a target; they were always aiming for targets. They gripped the steering wheel tight. Nothing distracted them, and they didn't look around.

On my way out I might have thrown the car keys into my jacket pocket this time, too, but a week on the road had been enough. I didn't want to see the car – I couldn't bear to see the car – so I walked.

* * *

It's not for no reason that human beings have lived for thousands of years on these high clay banks, not wishing to leave them. Whatever the circumstances – and at times the circumstances were gut-wrenching and life grew utterly unbearable – life has never been snuffed out. Something keeps us here, replenishing us with the force of life. Come what may, the force of life has always been abundant in the Kiev hills. But wisdom has been in short supply, that's for certain. The only ruler capable of introducing a more or less intelligible code of law was immediately christened 'the Wise', although his decision has always struck me not so much a demonstration of wisdom as ordinary common sense. Even now our common sense is in good order – that's pretty much always been the case, whoever the bosses may be, whoever is in charge. We're not strategic thinkers, so there are always people who want to think strategically for us, but when it comes to making perfect tactical decisions, our Ukrainian Yarik, salt-of-the-earth and worthy heir to Prince Yaroslav the Wise, is without rival. What this means, in effect, is that Yarik has corn and wheat in the threshing barn and potatoes and apples in the larder as well as sauerkraut and salted cucumbers, tomatoes and garlic and salted lard, of course; he's got a real beast in the stables and a young boar and a bull calf and a heifer; and in the little cellar he has moonshine for domestic needs and for settling up with workers for little jobs. He's got a good mate on the district council, and his brother works for the road patrol. On Sundays he goes to the bathhouse for a steam with the priest, and the son of the nouveau-very-riche 'New Ukrainian' from the next village has sent matchmakers to Galya, his eldest daughter. His own son is growing up and going to school, and when he finishes his studies he'll be just like his dad. What happened next was no longer his concern. That Vakha and his friends were already in Crimea in the brotherly company of their fellow Muslims, few but fervent, was not visible to him from behind his fence. And just what should he see? That Vakha was hauling nuts? Let him haul all the nuts he wants. Our fellow Yarik has a mate on the district council and a brother in the road patrol. If there's a problem, his brother will give Vakha a fine for a traffic offence.

Kurochkin, too, had been sure he was holding all the reins when – bam! – the ultimatum from his youth arrived by email and everything was turned upside down. Within two weeks he was a fugitive hiding in Israel and an exile . . . But what about our fellow Yarik? The time was coming when Vakha would say, 'Move over, Yarik, you're taking up too much room. I'm feeling hemmed in with you on my land', and he'll start shoving Yarik. First he'll push him out of Crimea, and next . . . we'll see what's next. And then what? His politically correct mate on the district council will suggest observing the right of nations to self-determination up to and including secession, and his brother the traffic cop would love to help, but he's getting old, and it seems he's got nothing left but his truncheon . . .

I roamed the city not thinking about anything. The thoughts came and went of their own accord, melting away into the fresh air of approaching spring. Empty thoughts.

Suddenly I found myself in front of the building where our firm had its tenth-floor offices. Although I hadn't meant to, somehow I'd ended up here, and the sooner I got away the better. But, as fate would have it, at the very moment I was trying to slip past the front door, a familiar automobile came to a halt right beside me. Steven Malkin in person climbed out of the car and took several brisk steps along the Kiev pavement. Half a second later we were standing eyeball to eyeball. I was not prepared to have a conversation with him and not at all happy about running into him. But Malkin, who wasn't expecting to bump into me either, seemed even less pleased.

'Well, well, Mr Davidov,' he bleated, swiftly leaping back a metre. 'Have you decided to honour your place of employment with a visit?'

Malkin shouldn't have done that. He should have walked right on past without even noticing me or with only the slightest of nods, so that I would spend the rest of the day wondering whether he had actually nodded or whether it had just seemed that way.

I didn't know what to say to my infuriated boss. That I was out for a walk in the middle of the work day while the rest of the office was labouring as one to increase profits? I had nothing to say to him. An unpleasant pause hung between us. People were staring. Malkin was on edge. An abnormal situation had developed, a situation not addressed in the NLP textbooks. The textbooks left no room for chance, but chance had turned up right before their eyes, right on the steps to the main entrance.

'During your absence,' said Malkin suddenly, grinding his teeth, 'during your prolonged absence, our situation, and yours, has undergone certain changes.' He tried to take himself in hand and worked his mouth into a smile. 'I'm taking advantage of this meeting to inform you that you can stop coming to work. As for details, you'll be informed in writing.'

Finally he feigned the slight nod he should have begun with and hastily disappeared behind the door.

Poor Malkin. He'd gone and broken yet another rule: never give bad news in person. The boss can congratulate you on your success or inform you of a promotion or pay rise, but the boss never tells you you're getting the sack or any other nasty news. That's the responsibility of the secretary who will write in evasive terms on headed paper: 'In the circumstances the company regrets to inform you that it will no longer require your . . .' But perhaps he wasn't poor Malkin, after all. Perhaps he had been dreaming about this moment, what he would say about the circumstances and the company no longer requiring . . . If so, one might feel a little sympathy for Malkin. Let's say he'd imagined all the details and fine points of what he would say to me, how my face would fall, how right before his eyes I would be transformed from a colleague in a major international firm, for less than five minutes the head of the Department of Microstrategic Planning, into your typical jobless Ukrainian. But being aware of his power wasn't enough for him; he wanted everyone around him to feel how powerful he was. And what had happened?

There in the damp wind at the door to the office building, beneath the surprised glances of the guards and chance passers-by, he hadn't managed more than a couple of pitiful sentences. He had missed a splendid opportunity. What a shame.

I wandered slowly onwards, contemplating Malkin's plight. I didn't know what had happened at the office over the past week. Perhaps I'd been sacked because of Kurochkin, or perhaps Kurochkin had nothing to do with it. In any case, Malkin had been a great help. I couldn't imagine returning to my desk, sitting down at the computer and commencing to draw up a strategy for selling cola. I simply couldn't imagine it. I'd already wasted five years on cola. Enough. And another thing. For some reason Malkin hadn't mentioned William F. Hume. There had been no reason to do so. But when had he ever needed a reason? That meant he was well and truly shaken.

* * *

At last I judged the protracted farewell with Malkin to be closed, and found myself walking along Bolshoi Zhytomyr Street. It was drizzling lightly, and dusk was approaching. I ran across the road, turned on to a back street and came out in the direction of Old Kiev Hill. Before me was Gonchari-Kozhumyaki. After a twenty-year hiatus development here had resumed in this old quarter. Beyond loomed Castle Hill. I breathed the damp spring air in deeply. It felt like it was starting to get warmer.

'It's warming up. Have you noticed?' said a voice behind me that I couldn't fail to recognize.

'The wind is changing. Are you still following me?'

'I haven't been following you, Alex, and I'm not going to start now.' Sinevusov came up and stood beside me.

'Then I suppose it's just your habit to walk here in the rain.' I nodded knowingly.

'So what if it's raining. I live here.' He waved towards Volodymyr Street. 'I'm walking my dog.'

I saw that Sinevusov had a lead in his hand.

'Which one's yours?' Near by a band of dogs was gambolling joyfully.

'No, mine's over there.' He pointed at a sad, solitary terrier negotiating the incline with difficulty. Sinevusov whistled and slapped his hand against his thigh. The terrier made as if it to race over to his owner, but it didn't gain any speed.

'A venerable old dog,' I concluded.

'No. Just cunning and lazy,' sniffed Sinevusov.

Slowly we made our way towards the History Museum.

'Well, seeing as how we've accidentally bumped into one another, it would be a shame not to ask you – did *you* let Kurochkin down, too?'

'What gives you that idea?' asked Sinevusov with genuine astonishment. 'That's not my style. Absolutely not. On the contrary, I'd have helped him for old times' sake. Although, like you, I could see early on that it was better to keep my distance. He let himself down, Alex, and that's the literal truth. It's all his own fault. Why do you think he called on a couple of old lags like you and me to help him? Do you think we two are uniquely qualified? You can be sure he's met far more qualified specialists in his time. Don't you reckon?'

'I don't doubt it.'

'And you shouldn't. There's just no one left he can trust. Kurochkin has managed to play the swine for everyone. For some he's just been a little piglet, for others a whopping great hog. Everyone except you and me, although . . . You, too, but you still don't seem to realize.'

'Leave it. If he were that much of a swine his true colours would be been shown by now. I'd know if he'd done anything.'

'Brace yourself then.' Sinevusov laughed softly. 'You're about to witness a showing of the colours, as they say. Anyway, it's an old story that has nothing to do with what's happening now – or maybe just a bit . . .' He laughed again.

'Go ahead, then.' I shrugged. 'Let your skeleton out of the closet and into the light of day.'

'You can call it a skeleton if you like, although I prefer something more neutral such as the history of an acquaintance, yours and mine.'

Sinevusov paused and stole a glance at me. I'd caught the hint. I'd understood him, and for a moment it took my breath away. It was impossible.

'Don't talk crap, Sinevusov. Kurochkin was detained for two months just like me. Just like all of us. We were

145

both expelled from university, and we were both sent into the army – him, too. Can't you come up with a better story than that? Do you really think I'm that stupid? I'm genuinely insulted.'

'He turned out to be a hulking fat boar of a swine.' He nodded contentedly. 'In fact it's incredible that he didn't manage to ruin things for you, Davidov. How have you ever managed to preserve your almost virgin purity and your trust in an old student friendship. You might have learned by now . . .'

'That's what I thought. You don't have any facts.'

'Facts, facts . . . Do you really need to see papers, eh? I don't carry them around with me, and I wasn't expecting to have this conversation, as I'm sure you can appreciate. But put your brain in gear, Davidov, and perhaps you can figure it out without documents. Let's begin with the fall-out. Kurochkin was the only one of you who managed to get back into university. And not just into a radiophysics department but a law department, after all that had happened . . . Moving on to your two years in the army. Those were two lost years for you but not for Kurochkin. He was working on his career. Can't you see? Even then. Step one: inform on a group of apolitical students who were quantitatively simulating the partition of the Soviet Union; step two: the army; step three: a law degree. He maintained contact with the KGB at all times. So, moving on . . . Although it's true that it had nothing to do with you personally. Incidentally, Davidov, have you ever played Civilization?'

'No, I'm not interested.'

'I suppose you had your fill when you were younger. I ask because your game was more fun to play. On the computer I'm building civilizations at 300-per-cent settings. Can you believe it? It draws you in, but it's not the same. You had real people playing. Psychology. A battle of minds . . .'

'Why did you let us go then if we were quantitatively simulating?'

'The winds were changing.'

'I thought we'd already talked about the weather.'

'I'm not talking about the weather. The first two or three weeks we were working you in the usual way when we got a command to slow down. So we slowed down. A week passed, then two, then three, then a month – how long could we keep it up? Then we got another command – let the pups go. And we let you go.'

'It would seem Kurochkin's efforts were in vain.'

'What's he got to do with it? He did his bit, there's no question about that. But the situation changed. You just got lucky.'

We had got as far the History Museum. The rain intensified. Sinevusov's terrier marked a pagan temple unearthed by the archaeologist Vikenty Khvoika more than a hundred years before and sat down for a good scratch. Spray flew from his withers in a wide arc.

'Step back,' said Sinevusov, taking me by the elbow. 'He's about to shake himself.'

'OK,' I said without comprehension. 'Let's say Kurochkin was responsible for what happened. But the four of us were the only ones affected. We were the only ones who even knew about it. So who's responsible for the letter? And the 90 million he can't account for?'

'Ah,' laughed Sinevusov, 'yes, the letter about the 90 million. It had to be edited somewhat. No, not me, I didn't tamper with it.' He waved and caught my eye. 'I only gave advice, although you can hardly call it advice. I contributed one short sentence to make it sound more plausible.'

'Yes,' I guessed. 'The YT at the bottom of the page. Your turn.'

'He was on edge because of the ultimatum, so I played along a little. I "stole the letter from his care and left a different letter there" as Pushkin once wrote.'

'Then the ultimatum was your work.'

'No.'

'Go ahead and lie if you want to. But why deny it when you've already told me everything? You're the only one who could have done it.'

'Why lie when all I have to do is keep quiet?'

'Then what are you telling me for?'

'I think you have a right to know what really happened. And I always thought you were a decent person.'

His compliments were lost on me. I didn't trust him.

'But', he went on, 'am I right to think that you still don't know who sent the ultimatum?'

'There's no one but you,' I repeated stubbornly.

'I see. You don't know. I'm asking not because it's

important or might change anything but because there's still one final link missing.'

'You want closure?'

'Of course I do.'

Night was rolling in upon the city, and the rain had begun to pour down more heavily. I watched Castle Hill receding into darkness – and I was back there, one bright day in May. I saw Kurochkin and myself. Only the night before we'd been released from Volodymyr Street, he had left Ryskalov; I, Sinevusov. We'd been victors then, that was obvious, and now Sinevusov was telling me there had been no victory. I gave him a quick glance. He, too, was looking at Castle Hill, but I couldn't begin to imagine what he was thinking. A large drop of rain quivered on his temple and trickled down his cheek. He used to sweat oil. Oil and venom. His deepest, innermost thoughts surfaced as oil and venom. But now it was water. Nothing but rainwater.

The rain poured down, washing away the remnants of colours we'd once used to paint over this dismal landscape. The water was ruthless and stubborn in its insistence on absolute truth.

Suddenly I recalled my previous meeting with Sinevusov.

'Do you remember the café last week in Podol? There was this bloke you were trying to recruit.'

'I wasn't trying to recruit him. I'll bet he was English.'

'So you remember. I wanted to ask what you said to him after I left.'

'So you noticed, eh? That's OK. It wasn't anything major. I said we'd blown his cover a long time ago – and I said you were the Russian FSB colonel charged with liquidating him.'

'Fantastic. What did you do that for?'

'So he'd step more lively. He was acting so lethargic it irritated me just looking at him.'

'Well, of course, in that case . . .'

'We should be getting home,' said Sinevusov and whistled to his dog. 'How can I get in touch with you? Have you got an email address?'

'Why don't you write it down. Have you got a pen?'

'Just tell me – I'll remember.'

'It's Istemi at –'

'Is what?'

'You'd better write it down. I'll spell it. I-S-T-E –'

'Ah, I get it.' Sinevusov laughed. 'Istemi, of course . . . What was it you called yourself? The Khan of the Zaporozhian Encampment? I remember now. That's just what I needed to learn it by. But let me know if you find out who sent the ultimatum.'

'I will.'

'I'm easy to find. I go for a walk every evening.' He gave me a slight wave goodbye.

Sinevusov and his mournful terrier went off towards Volodymyr Street, and I continued to stand there, getting soaked and studying the views of night-time Kiev. It was time for me to go, too.

* * *

When I'd left home that morning to spend a couple of hours wandering undisturbed around the city, I could not have imagined where, when and with whom I would finish my walk. It wouldn't be hard to ascribe some sort of mystical or symbolic meaning to what happened – if you wanted to. But I didn't want to. Once upon a time we had brought forth shadows, and those shadows ended up changing our lives – it was our own fault, no one else's. To this day those shadows had not dissipated. They were still Emperor of the Holy Roman Empire Karl XX, President of the Slovenorussian Federation Stefan Betancourt, President of the United Islamic Caliphates Caliph Al-Ali, Lama of Mongolia Undur Gegen, Istemi Khan of the Khanate of Zaporozhye and Major Sinevusov of the Committee for State Security. And although their hold on us was not what it used to be – it had grown weaker over the years and would grow weaker still – it would never completely leave us. The way the memory of one hot day in May 1984 spent by Kurochkin and me on Castle Hill would never leave me. It was the day we had won. If anyone should ask me about the happiest day of my life, I know what my answer will always be.

I was standing opposite Castle Hill, but the hill was already disappearing into night – I could make out only its silhouette – and beyond the hill, beyond Podol, in the Kurenyovka district, was the hospital where Reingarten was kept, where I hadn't gone to see him. On that May day, he also believed we had won.

* * *

My mobile was vibrating in my jacket pocket.

'Have you really been sleeping all day?' Vera asked.

'No, I didn't lie in.'

'Then why didn't you call?'

'I thought you were sleeping. I didn't want to wake you.'

'Yes, I was sleeping,' she said contentedly. 'Until lunch. But now I've caught up. And do you know what I did when I woke up?'

'What did you do?'

'I called Natasha *née* Belokrinitskaya.'

'What for?' I was surprised.

'Just because. To make sure her number hadn't changed. After all, I said I'd give it to you.'

'Thanks. Although I don't think I'll have any use for it now. How is she?'

'She has no complaints. She remembers you, and the others, too. And you know what else she said? That she was the one who sent that letter to Kurochkin and the rest of you. With the ultimatum.'

'Natasha? But why?' I looked, but Sinevusov had already vanished into the darkness. I had no intention of telling him anyway.

'No special reason. She was just having a bit of fun. She wanted to play a joke on you all.'

'Really?' I asked stupidly. 'A joke? It was one hell of a prank.'

'She was going through some old papers a few months ago and came across the draft ultimatum. It made her think about old times, lost youth and all that, so she typed up the text. And when she came to the date, well, exactly twenty years had passed, so she wrote an email, sent it to Kurochkin and copied it to the rest of you.'

'Astonishing.' I shook my head, great big drops of water flying off of me just like Sinevusov's dog. 'It's the most brilliant practical joke I've ever heard of.'

'I told her that. I said that over here people had taken her joke very seriously and that Kurochkin had jumped ship altogether and hightailed it to the Holy Land. To atone for his sins. Isn't that right?'

'That's it exactly. You've captured the nuances very well.'

'Don't tease. So where are you?'

I looked at the empty rain-filled streets of the neighbourhood.

'The centre, Vera. I'm in the centre without a car. Are you at home?'

'Yes, at home.'

'Never mind, I'll think of something.'

'Have a think,' said Vera easily. 'I'm sure you'll think of something.'

* * *

Our talk was long overdue. We should have spoken before all the madness in the hours before his departure when he'd started sending me terse emails asking me to get in touch urgently. Or later, after I'd talked to Sinevusov, and Kurochkin had already gone and stopped making demands. There had been plenty of time to dial his number, but still I put it off.

Ten days after our return from Crimea Vera left as planned to spend a year in Germany. I'd already received her first letters. After the buzz of life in Kiev, so bright and busy, she was finding it hard to get used to the quiet, deliberate, unhurried way of life in Lindau – twenty minutes from Hettingen, an hour from Hanover and two hours from Frankfurt.

Even before Vera left an email had arrived from Natasha. I opened it with a superstitious shudder that surprised me. This Hotmail address was all too familiar. It was from this address that the letter signed by Emperor Karl had come on 9 March. It was difficult for me to read it; I'm sure it was no easier to write it.

'I could hardly believe that what I'd thought was such a harmless little joke could set such events into motion,' she wrote.

I have to admit that I didn't believe Vera at first. I thought you just wanted to play a joke on me in return. It wasn't until I'd gone through dozens of Ukrainian news sites that I could see she wasn't making it up. And she might not have told me everything at that. Vera asked me to tell you how I got hold of the text. There's not a lot to say. Korostishevski had borrowed my notes on the history of the party (I can't even remember any more which of these words is capitalized – or perhaps they both are?) and misplaced them. He looked for them, but when he couldn't find them he thought they

154

must be in the folder Nedremailo had taken from him. It was obviously going to be easier for me to talk to Nedremailo – he was a relative after all, and we'd always got on well. Can you imagine how surprised I was when Nedremailo wouldn't let me look in the folder, not even in his presence? He just said my notes weren't there and told me to stop playing games with him. I remember being astonished and full of indignation at the time, and I decided to take a look myself. I staged quite a production to get my hands on that folder. I went back one morning a few days later. The only person at home was his wife, Elena Vasilievna, Vera's mother. To distract her I asked my mother to give her a ring at a prearranged time. While they were chatting I found the folder and went through everything inside it. He was right when he said my notes weren't there. I'd gone to such lengths and all for nothing. Then I took out one of the drafts of the ultimatum – there was more than one in the folder – and a couple of pages copied from a collection of pre-Revolutionary documents. As a trophy. I looked at it more carefully when I got home. It was the ultimatum made by Austria-Hungary to the Serbs in July 1914. Korostishevski had just amended it a little.

Then you all were arrested, and I was left without my notes. I should mention that Nedremailo figured out I'd been rifling through the folder, but he never mentioned it. And that's the whole story.

'You know, Alex,' Natasha went on, and I really felt that I could hear her voice,

I've been thinking about all of you quite a lot of late, the way you were all chasing after me, trying to not give yourselves away but trying to get my attention at the same time. Usually we reminisce when things aren't going too well – although things are going quite well for me – but it's not nostalgia either. Far from it. It's just that it was such a long time ago. Rather, it seemed like such a long time ago, I felt sure of that. But, you see, time has ended up being finer than a thin sheet of paper. It only takes a little pressure and, there you go, the past is right beside you. Maybe time isn't real at all. Maybe we've only invented it.'

* * *

Kurochkin rang. In the morning the phone began tinkling delicately. I picked up the receiver and he said, 'Hi, Alex, how goes it? Kurochkin here.'

'Hi, Kurochkin. Every day I've been meaning to call you . . .'

'How could you? I've changed my numbers. I've changed everything – from my wife to my country. Just joking. A new and wonderful life is just waiting.'

'Why change everything? What with your parlia - mentary immunity –'

'Davidov, don't start. I've already thought, changed my mind and changed my mind again. Of course, I could have stood my ground and fought back, I could have pulled rank, but what for? They would have crushed me all the same. And it would have been more painful. For me and everyone around me, including you.

In short, I'm OK now. What about you? I looked for you before I left. I wanted to tell you it was all off – the searches, investigations, all those letters, ultimatums – it's a false trail, a deception. I wanted to tell you to lie low for a while until everything got back to normal, to go away somewhere. So, then, how are you doing? What have you been up to?'

'Well, I'm not selling water any more if that's what you want to know.'

Kurochkin understood. 'So Malkin gave you the sack, did he? You should have expected as much. It's not such a bad thing – it's even good. You're a free man now. We have something in common to commiserate over . . . Have you had any other problems?'

'Nothing new.'

'So everything's all right then? Hey, what do you mean by "new"?'

'I saw Sinevusov a few days ago. He said that back in '84 you were the one who reported us to Volodymyr Street.'

'Ah, yes. It was me,' he confirmed tersely.

'So just what can the two of us have in common, Kurochkin?' I asked after a short pause.

'Alex, hang on. I've been wanting to tell you everything for a long time. It was me, yes, but what can I do about it now? Forgive me. I was an idiot, a boy. I didn't understand the gravity of what I was doing. I didn't understand what it was going to cost. And then . . . well, it all went wrong. One thing on top of another. It's weighed on me all my life, and I didn't know how to tell you. And now you can see for yourself how it's ended.'

'Kanyuka is complaining about you,' I went on. 'He says you ruined him.'

'You don't hit a man when he's already down, do you? It was Kanyuka's own fault. He shouldn't have been so greedy. I felt no obligation towards him, but you . . . I swear to you, I always meant to . . . Back then I planned to give everyone a hand and make up for what I'd done. You don't know it, but I even went to Nedremailo to get the file he'd taken from Sashka Korostishevski.'

'I do know.'

'Then you know I'm not lying. But he wouldn't give it to me. That's when I realized Nedremailo was going to turn us in.'

'And you wanted to get a jump on him.' I laughed.

'At the very least so I could pave the way and make it a little easier on everyone.'

'Yes, of course. By the way, I found out who sent you the ultimatum.'

'What does it matter now? What? Really? It wasn't one of Sinevusov's cronies? Then who was it?'

'Guess.' I suddenly felt unbearably hot. I could hardly breathe. One bead of sweat trickled swiftly from temple to chin, followed by another. 'You ought to remember this person well.'

'What? Who?' Kurochkin stammered helplessly. 'Who was it?'

I almost said, 'Sashka Korostishevski has come back,

and he wants to see you. He wants to finish the game. And the rest of the guys wouldn't mind seeing you either.'

I should have said it. I really should. Instead I drew a deep breath and told him about the email from Belokrinitskaya.

'That is absolutely mad,' he was saying a minute later, gasping from laugher. 'I mean, really? Belokrinitskaya? That has got to be the funniest thing I've heard in my life. Just think. Classy, huh? Who'd have thought?'

I was no longer listening. I put the receiver down and rubbed my face, trying to wipe away the sweat. But my palms just slid across my cheeks, spreading oil and venom.

SOME AUTHORS WE HAVE PUBLISHED

James Agee • Bella Akhmadulina • Tariq Ali • Kenneth Allsop • Alfred Andersch
Guillaume Apollinaire • Machado de Assis • Miguel Ángel Asturias • Duke of Bedford
Oliver Bernard • Thomas Blackburn • Jane Bowles • Paul Bowles • Richard Bradford
Ilse, Countess von Bredow • Lenny Bruce • Finn Carling • Blaise Cendrars • Marc Chagall
Giorgio de Chirico • Uno Chiyo • Hugo Claus • Jean Cocteau • Albert Cohen
Colette • Ithell Colquhoun • Richard Corson • Benedetto Croce • Margaret Crosland
e.e. cummings • Stig Dalager • Salvador Dali • Osamu Dazai • Anita Desai
Charles Dickens • Bernard Diederich • Fabián Dobles • William Donaldson
Autran Dourado • Yuri Druzhnikov • Lawrence Durrell • Isabelle Eberhardt
Sergei Eisenstein • Shusaku Endo • Erté • Knut Faldbakken • Ida Fink
Wolfgang George Fischer • Nicholas Freeling • Philip Freund • Carlo Emilio Gadda
Rhea Galanaki • Salvador Garmendia • Michel Gauquelin • André Gide
Natalia Ginzburg • Jean Giono • Geoffrey Gorer • William Goyen • Julien Gracq
Sue Grafton • Robert Graves • Angela Green • Julien Green • George Grosz
Barbara Hardy • H.D. • Rayner Heppenstall • David Herbert • Gustaw Herling
Hermann Hesse • Shere Hite • Stewart Home • Abdullah Hussein • King Hussein of Jordan
Ruth Inglis • Grace Ingoldby • Yasushi Inoue • Hans Henny Jahnn • Karl Jaspers
Takeshi Kaiko • Jaan Kaplinski • Anna Kavan • Yasunuri Kawabata • Nikos Kazantzakis
Orhan Kemal • Christer Kihlman • James Kirkup • Paul Klee • James Laughlin
Patricia Laurent • Violette Leduc • Lee Seung-U • Vernon Lee • József Lengyel
Robert Liddell • Francisco García Lorca • Moura Lympany • Dacia Maraini
Marcel Marceau • André Maurois • Henri Michaux • Henry Miller • Miranda Miller
Marga Minco • Yukio Mishima • Quim Monzó • Margaret Morris • Angus Wolfe Murray
Atle Næss • Gérard de Nerval • Anaïs Nin • Yoko Ono • Uri Orlev • Wendy Owen
Arto Paasilinna • Marco Pallis • Oscar Parland • Boris Pasternak • Cesare Pavese
Milorad Pavic • Octavio Paz • Mervyn Peake • Carlos Pedretti • Dame Margery Perham
Graciliano Ramos • Jeremy Reed • Rodrigo Rey Rosa • Joseph Roth • Ken Russell
Marquis de Sade • Cora Sandel • George Santayana • May Sarton • Jean-Paul Sartre
Ferdinand de Saussure • Gerald Scarfe • Albert Schweitzer • George Bernard Shaw
Isaac Bashevis Singer • Patwant Singh • Edith Sitwell • Suzanne St Albans • Stevie Smith
C.P. Snow • Bengt Söderbergh • Vladimir Soloukhin • Natsume Soseki • Muriel Spark
Gertrude Stein • Bram Stoker • August Strindberg • Rabindranath Tagore
Tambimuttu • Elisabeth Russell Taylor • Emma Tennant • Anne Tibble • Roland Topor
Miloš Urban • Anne Valery • Peter Vansittart • José J. Veiga • Tarjei Vesaas
Noel Virtue • Max Weber • Edith Wharton • William Carlos Williams • Phyllis Willmott
G. Peter Winnington • Monique Wittig • A.B. Yehoshua • Marguerite Young
Fakhar Zaman • Alexander Zinoviev • Emile Zola

www.peterowen.com